About the Author

Blanche Dabney is the author of the bestselling Clan MacGregor books, a series of sweet and clean time travel romances set in medieval Scotland.

Growing up in a small village on the west coast of Scotland, Blanche spent many happy childhood hours exploring ancient castles, all the while inventing tall tales of the people who might once have lived there.

After years of wishing she could travel through time to see how accurate her stories were, she decided to do the next best thing, write books about the past.

Her first romance, Highlander's Voyage, came out in 2018, and reader reaction was positive enough for her to dedicate herself full time to writing more.

Since then, she has published more than half a dozen highland adventures, each filled with passion, danger, and intrigue.

Blanche lives in Haworth, home of the Bronte sisters, with her partner and their two children.

instagram.com/blanchedabneyauthor

amazon.com/author/blanchedabney

bookbub.com/authors/blanche-dabney

Also by Blanche Dabney

The Clan MacGregor Series

Medieval Highlander Trilogy

Highlander's Time Trilogy

The Clan MacGregor Series

The Key in the Loch

When a mysterious key sends Rachel Fisher back through time she arrives during a violent time in Scottish history. Her only hope of survival lies with grizzled medieval warrior, Cam MacGregor.

The Key in the Door

To save her life, Jessica Abrahams must convince everyone in the clan she is the missing fiancée of the laird.

The Key to Her Heart

Daisy Stone doesn't believe in love stories. But when she steps into the past she discovers the one man who might be able to give her a happy ending of her own.

The Key to Her Past

Natalie MacCallister lands in medieval Scotland in time to change history for the better.

THE KEY IN THE LOCH

A Scottish Time Travel Romance

BLANCHE DABNEY

BLANCHE
DABNEY

TIME TRAVEL ROMANCE

For Ellen

Chapter One

When the parcel arrived, Rachel
Fisher was lost in a book. She was
happily learning more about
medieval Scotland, black coffee going cold at her
side. All was right with the world. Until the knock
on the door.

Knock.

She marked her place with a bookmark -
Benson's, best for books - and then added the tome to
the already tottering pile on her coffee table. Two
weeks left to get through the entire lot.

From where she was sitting she could read the
spines of them all. Norman Chivalry, The Golden
Age, Hardmann's Scottish Clans, The Wars of

Independence. All of them four hundred pages plus. A fortnight to finish them all if she wanted to be prepared when her Masters began.

If only she hadn't been distracted by all the other books over the summer, the ones where knights rescued fair maidens, and the more modern ones where the maidens didn't need rescuing, thank you very much.

The ones filled with romance that the dry histories of real Scotland could never hope to match. The factual accounts were all, "The Laird married the lady," and then onto the next generation.

Where was the passion? The wooing? The coy glances across a packed hall? Reality could never match fiction for such things. Maybe she should have studied English Lit instead of Medieval History.

Maybe she shouldn't have taken on a Masters at all. Stayed at the supermarket and settled into the management trainee course like they wanted her to. She wasn't sure why she was doing the Masters. What she really wanted was to book a ticket to the Middle Ages. Studying it was the next best thing.

She just needed to focus. Ignore all distractions. Which would be a lot easier if someone wasn't knocking loudly on the door.

She had started that morning on page one of Hardmann's Scottish Clans. She was halfway through and boning up on the MacGregors when the knock on the door rattled her concentration. The clan was wiped out in the twelfth century but no one knew why. There was a single mention of a barefoot man but it meant nothing to Rachel.

She got up to answer the door and, at the same time, her cell phone rang. She crammed the cell against her shoulder while heading into the hallway.

"Hello?"

"You've not forgotten, have you?"

"Ah, the dulcet tones of my ever-furious brother. How are you Alan?" She pulled the door open as he continued. A mailman she didn't recognise was standing there with a scowl on his face that matched her brother's tone of voice. She nodded to him, taking the parcel he thrust into her hand as Alan continued berating her down the phone-line.

"I can't believe you've forgotten. The one thing you had to do was turn up and you can't even be bothered. Christ, Rachel, I don't even know why I'm surprised."

"What?" she asked, pushing the front door closed and returning to the living room, dropping the parcel on top of her pile of books. "What have I forgotten?"

She glanced at the parcel. It was wrapped in tartan paper, red and black, a pattern she recognized but she wasn't sure where from.

The twine that held it closed had come undone and the paper was unfurling like the petals of a flower, revealing a small dark wooden box. The wood was so dark it looked black.

Alan said something she didn't hear. She was distracted by the intricate M carved into the lid of the box. It looked exactly like the MacGregor seal she'd only just seen in Hardmann's.

Her finger ran over the letter. Before she knew what was happening, a jolt of electricity sparked from the box, leaping across to her hand. From outside a gust of wind blew in, sending the curtains billowing upward. The air smelled of heather.

Alan was still ranting but had yet to get to the point. "I can't believe you need to ask. Are you just doing this to wind me up, is that it? If you think you're getting the house, you've got another thing coming. You never cared about her. Why would she leave you anything?"

"Alan, will you wipe the rabid foam from your

mouth and start talking sense. What are you on about?"

Reaching down, she tried to open the box. It was locked. Rummaging in the packaging, she saw no sign of a key, or a note.

Who had sent her a box that couldn't be opened?

"Your mother's funeral."

"Sorry, Alan," she said, the box forgotten. "Say that again."

"Your own mother's funeral and you forget. I mean I know I shouldn't be surprised. You never once picked up the phone to find out how she's been doing."

"Funeral? You mean she's dead?"

"Of course she's dead. Are you going to pretend you didn't get my email?"

"I didn't get it."

"Of course you didn't. Stop the bull, Rachel, and admit you forgot because you don't give a toss about her."

"I didn't know, I swear."

"Yeah, right."

"Look, when is it?"

"Two o'clock at St Mary's."

"I'll be there."

Alan hung up. She was glad. He would only get louder. She had absolutely no doubt that he hadn't sent an email. If he had sent it, she'd have seen it at once on her cellphone. No, he'd waited until the day of the funeral so he could be sure to catch her on the back foot. Just like him.

She idly ran her finger over the burns on her arms. She'd told him about them, about what Julia had done and what had he done? Told her she deserved it.

Now she had to decide quickly whether or not to go.

Turning away from the living room, she ran through to the bedroom, already thinking about what to wear. There weren't many etiquette guides she could refer to.

Dear Cosmo, What should I wear to the funeral of my adoptive mother who hated me and was so cruel to me for all those years until I finally got it together to leave and never look back? The woman who I keep expecting to appear over my shoulder at any moment, the one who ruined any chance I had of a normal life. The one who made it impossible for me to love anyone or anything? Any advice? Ah, dark gray knee length dress. Great, got it.

She stopped dead in the middle of the bedroom. Should she go? She hadn't seen Julia since when? Gosh, since she was sixteen. That was eleven years ago. She hadn't spoken to Alan in more than two years. The last time was when she found out Julia was ill.

She tried to go visit. Julia wouldn't let her inside. If she'd had her way she would have only adopted Alan and left Rachel to rot in the children's home. It was only because Mrs. Dalrymple had insisted the two of them remain together that Julia took them both in.

For her entire time in that house Rachel paid dearly for that. While Alan was doted upon, she, to put it bluntly, was not.

She shook her head. She should still go, if only for his sake. He was still her brother and he was grieving for a woman he loved. She could support him. Or he might kill her for actually turning up.

She smiled at the thought of a murder at a funeral. Maybe they'd get two for one, chuck an extra body into the furnace. She winced. Inappropriate joke. Better get them all out of the way before she got there. No one would appreciate her dark sense of humor. They might roast her for it.

Right, that's enough, she told herself. No more awful jokes. Focus.

She pulled open the wardrobe and worked her way through the coat hangers. There wasn't a black dress in sight. How had she made it to twenty-seven years old without buying a single black dress?

There was a black skirt but it was nightclub length. Not really suitable when she wanted to try and patch things up with her brother. He'd take one look and the word slut would fall out of his mouth before he even knew he was saying it.

She kept looking. If only he knew how far from the truth his insults had always been. She, who had never slept with anyone in her entire life, accused of whoring herself around so often, she almost thought it was true.

Stop it, stop thinking about the past. Get into the mourning mindset. Imagine it was the funeral of your actual mother, not the one who kept you locked in your room whenever you weren't at school.

Charcoal gray trousers.

They'd do. Thin for a chilly May but she wouldn't be outside for long.

White blouse?

No, she'd look like she was part of the catering team for the wake.

What about that?

A black top, scooped neck, not too revealing, not even a hint of the cleavage she didn't have. Long sleeves which would help if the cold wind kept blowing. The wool coat from goodwill would keep her warm enough if it did.

What shoes to wear with it?

The flat Chelsea boots would be best. No one would appreciate Converse with Calvin and Hobbes handpainted on the sides.

Decision made, she dressed quickly and was out the door ten minutes later. Quick check of her cell-phone. Fifty percent battery. It should be more than enough to survive there and back again.

There were no seats on the train. She stood crammed in the corridor, looking out through the window at the city passing by in a blur. An hour to get to Haworth and then a short walk up the hill to the church. Plenty of time to try and summon up some emotions other than empty sickness.

It shouldn't be so hard. Julia brought her up. She must be able to find some sorrow somewhere inside her. She tried starting with Haworth.

She only had to close her eyes to picture the

walk between the train station and the cobbled Main Street. She'd done it so often during her childhood, sent off to the shops in nearby Keighley because Julia needed something urgently, though not urgently enough to go in her car and get it herself. It was the only time she was allowed out of her room except to go to school.

"Good exercise for you," Julia would say, poking Rachel in the stomach. "Get rid of some of that puppy fat. No man'll want you if you don't lose some of that weight."

And there in a nutshell was the reason for the eating disorder she was still recovering from. What would Alan think when he saw her? She looked better than she had in years but she still considered herself too thin.

Could she ever be happy by herself? An entire childhood being told she was too fat until she believed it, and then once she'd moved away, losing so much weight she was almost hospitalized. And then years of worrying she was too thin and finally, very slowly, putting the weight back on.

That was part of why she was permanently cold. No insulating layer of fat. Just skin and bone. The other reason she was always cold was because spring had decided to have a lie in and was showing no signs of getting up any time soon.

It had been raining for a solid week and when it finally stopped that morning it was only to let the wind tag in for a while. The flowers outside the train window were wilting, Rachel knew how they felt. She would have killed for a little bit of sunshine.

Chapter Two

Rachel arrived in Haworth ten minutes late. When the train finally rolled into the station, she stepped off onto the platform and shivered. The wind tried to blow her back onboard. She almost let it.

Haworth. The place she swore she'd never return to. She could feel herself regressing with every step out of the station. One step for each year. Soon she'd be no more than a child again, waiting to get home and find out just what she'd done wrong this time.

The old fear was returning. Wondering what mood Julia would be in when she got there. Whether it would be silence, ear splitting yelling, or worse, cloying over-familiarity.

They were the hardest days. Julia sneaking into her room to whisper slurred beer smelling words to her, another man heading out the front door downstairs.

"You'll understand when you're my age." Her voice low and conspiratorial. "Men are wicked, Rachel, did you know that? They do disgusting things if you let them. You try to be good but they don't listen. They're awful and they stink too. Keep away from men, Rachel. Don't you worry, I'll protect you from them all."

She climbed the hill toward the church, trying but failing to shake the past from her mind. You could never wipe the slate clean.

Three years of university and now the Masters and still she felt like an imposter, like someone was about to grab her and tell her she was actually eight years old, what did she think she was doing pretending to be an adult?

It was time to go home and do her chores like a good girl. Stop thinking about the Middle Ages.

She realized she was hunching her shoulders as she walked. Even her posture was returning to how it used to be. She stood up deliberately tall, looking in at the park as she passed it.

The bandstand was still there. She remembered

sitting there with her few things in a carrier bag, weeping as she waited for the train, knowing she was never ever going back.

Until today.

As she crossed over the road to Main Street, she found herself, out of nowhere, thinking about her birth mother. Was she still alive somewhere? Was her father?

It seemed unlikely. She had done her best to track them down over the years but the records didn't seem to exist. As far as the authorities were concerned, Rachel and Alan had simply appeared in a cabbage patch, dropped by a stork without any input from anyone human at all.

The one thing she wanted more than anything else was to find out who her parents were. The woman they were about to bid farewell to was not her mother. Not even close. She was as far from a mother as someone could be.

So why was she was going to her funeral? Was it really for Alan? She stopped dead in the middle of the street as she suddenly realized what it was. It was to make sure she was really gone. That she couldn't hurt her anymore.

"Wow," she said out loud as she continued on

her way up the steep hill to the church. "I really am damaged."

The mourners were few and as gray as Rachel's coat. She didn't recognize anyone except her brother. Even he'd changed since she'd last seen him. He'd put on a lot of weight.

"Nice beard," she said when she reached him at the top of the church steps. "Got a great homeless vibe to it. I almost gave you my spare change before I realized it was you."

"As witty as ever." He looked surprised to see her. "You made it then."

"I thought you might want me here. Make up the numbers."

"Of course," he said, his face saying the opposite. "Shall we go in?"

The mourners had left space on the front row. They sat listening as the priest began to talk about a woman she didn't recognize, a good woman, a kind woman who would be missed by the entire community.

She wondered if she would cry. Some of the others were crying. Alan was wracked with uncontrollable sobs. She looked at him, thinking again about the differences between the two of them. A couple of tutors at college had suggested she might be autistic. Unemotional, analytical, obsessive about her interests, few friends. Seeing his emotions tearing through him and observing them coldly, she felt more detached from humanity than ever.

How much grief was one supposed to feel? What was the right amount? If she threw herself on the floor and cursed God for taking Julia away would that make her a better or worse person in the eyes of everyone there?

There wasn't the sense of release she had expected from being there. It was as if her subconscious thought this might all be a test, that Julia still might rise up and point in her direction, tell her to get to Keighley to fetch twenty Marlboro and one of her gossip magazines.

When the coffin was carried out at the end of the service she found herself crying. She wasn't even sure why. Alan gave her a look as he went by. It was hard to tell whether it was approval or disgust. Either way she found herself crying harder.

The wake was held at Julia's house. She walked there alone, taking her time, falling behind the others, waiting for the crying to stop. She thought how mad she must look to the day-trippers who were walking down Main Street. "I just really love Wuthering Heights," she said to one couple who wouldn't stop staring at her as she cried. She tapped her heart. "Gets me right here."

She giggled through her tears before continuing downhill, leaving their bewildered faces behind. At the bottom of the street there was a house that stood apart from the terraced cottages. Her childhood home.

She stopped outside and gave herself a pep talk. You're an adult. She's definitely dead. She can't hurt you anymore. She can't lock you in your room. She can't even keep you out of the parlor anymore. If you want to go in there with muddy boots on and smear filth all along the sofa she can't do anything about it.

She'd often fantasised as a child about doing that, going in the forbidden room. She always told herself one day she'd be brave enough to do it. To stand up to her in the most pointless way by getting mud on the parlor carpet.

Now she could do it, she didn't want to. She just wanted to get it over with. Say goodbye to Alan, maybe for the last time. Then go back to her life. Medieval history. A lot less complicated than real life. For one thing, everyone was already dead. For another, people would find it pretty hard to yell at her from inside the pages of a textbook. The past was safe. Everyone in it was long dead.

A couple of people in black suits were smoking outside the front door, talking to each other in low voices. She passed between them and then inside. Alan was standing in the parlor, glass of whisky in his right hand. "She always loved this room," he told an approving gaggle of mourners. "It was her favorite space. Just like her, gentle and warm."

She walked past, heading upstairs to her old bedroom. Pushing the door open, she wasn't surprised to find it crammed with damp cardboard that had an overwhelming smell of must and mildew.

The smell of her childhood. Damp boxes. The room had been filled with boxes when she was there. Julia had just shoved some aside to fit a bed in. That was all she got. A bed and a single thin blanket. No pillow. No sheet. Just the blanket.

In fact, there was the blanket, still in the corner, buried underneath a mountain of stuff.

She casually looked into a couple of the boxes. Alistair MacClean novels, camping equipment that had never been used (all still with tags on), VHS videos with peeling labels. The writing had been crossed out multiple times. She'd recorded so many programs, never getting round to watching any of them.

She shoved some boxes aside so she could perch on the edge of the bed, feeling herself suffocating, needing to take a breath. As she sat down the precarious tower of stuff next to her creaked and then began to fall, landing with a thud on the floor, spilling contents everywhere. The room didn't look much different than before.

Alan appeared a few seconds later, leaning in the doorway. "What was that noise?"

"Some of the boxes fell over."

"Oh." He looked as if he was trying to decide what to say. "She used this room as storage after you went."

"She used it for storage when I was here."

"Look at that." Alan was pointing at something the other side of her.

One of the boxes had come to rest upside down, the contents sticking out onto the floor. Rachel looked, noticing a flash of the same tartan she'd seen just that morning. "What is that?"

"Oh my God," he said, kneeling down and pulling a tartan blanket out of the box, "I remember this. Mom left it for me."

"What?" Rachel said, picking up an envelope from next to the box. "As in our Mom?"

"It was on the doorstep. I was about seven, you would have been what, five? Julia said we could see it after school but when we got back she said she'd made a mistake, that it had gone back to the sender. She never told me she'd kept it. I knew it had come from Mom. I could just tell. What's that?"

Rachel had the envelope open. "It's a letter, to the two of us."

"Who from?"

"It's from Mom." Her voice almost broke but she managed to read the letter aloud. "Dear Alan and Rachel. One day you'll understand why it had to be this way. Please forgive me." She had to stop, tears blurring her eyes.

Alan snatched the letter from her, reading the rest while she looked over his shoulder. "The blanket is yours Alan. Rachel, the key is from the loch." He paused. "Of course it's from a lock. It's a key. Duh!"

"Loch," Rachel replied. "It's spelled L-O-C-H. Loch. As in Scottish lake."

"I knew that. What else does it say? That, and the necklace, are for you when you're older. You'll know how to use them when the time comes. I know you both have a lot of questions and I will answer them one day but not now. It's not the right time for me or you. I love you both. Mom."

Rachel picked up the fallen box and looked inside. At the bottom was a small silver key, the metalwork marked with the swirling M she'd already seen twice that day. There was no sign of a necklace, either in the box or on the floor, no matter how much she rummaged.

"What's that key for?" Alan asked as she continued to search.

"I've no idea."

Alan opened his mouth as if to say something, then seemed to notice he was pressing the blanket to his cheek. He coughed, shaking his head before putting the blanket back inside the box. "We should go back downstairs," he said, shoving the letter into his pocket. "Let the past be the past."

"Can I see the letter again?"

"No point, Rachel. It'll only upset you."

"I want to see it anyway."

"I said no," he snapped. "She's dead and this is just your pathetic attempt to get me worked up. It won't work. The will says I get the house and you can't do anything about that so don't even bother."

"I don't want the house, Alan. I just want to see the letter, please."

"No. Why did you have to come and rake up the past? Why couldn't you just let things lie?"

"You invited me, remember? Say goodbye to our mother."

"And you never came to see her while she was ill."

"I tried. She wouldn't let me in."

"You always hated her." He was spitting the words out, his face bright red.

"That's not true."

"Get out."

"What?"

He lowered his voice to a whisper, "You don't get the house, I do. I win." He pulled the letter out of his pocket and, as she reached out to it, he began tearing it into shreds, the pieces falling to the floor like confetti. "She abandoned us. You should stop worshipping her like that."

"Why did you do that?" she asked as he smiled coldly at her.

"Because I always win. She loved me, not you and you can't take it."

He turned away, walking slowly downstairs and leaving her alone. She knelt, picking up the pieces of the letter but the only word she could make out was love. She pressed the fragment to her heart before slipping it into her coat pocket.

Why was he like that? Why was he so filled with hatred. She had heard him rant so many times when they were children. We were abandoned. Julia is our mother now. She responded in kind. She loved him. She did not love Rachel. Would she ever understand why?

She only had to close her eyes to remember lying on that bed and sobbing, the nail marks on her arms stinging but hurting nowhere near as much as the feeling of being unwanted.

By the time she went downstairs Alan was nowhere to be seen. Nor were any of the other mourners. The house was empty. She looked outside. A group of them were heading up Main Street to The Fleece.

She guessed she wasn't invited. That was probably for the best.

She looked around the house one last time. Would Alan continue living in it? Sell it?

She sighed, pulling the door closed. She found she didn't care. Let him do what he wanted. She had a sign that her mother was real. She had lived and she had loved them both. It wasn't much but it was enough.

Alan had torn up the letter but he couldn't tear up the key as easily. She had an actual gift from their mother. He had the house of their adoptive mother. No doubt he believed he'd got the better deal.

She stood on the door step, having the strangest feeling that she would never set foot in there ever again.

She walked briskly back down to the train station, the key safely tucked away in her coat pocket. Her mom had loved her, had loved them both. She had the word in her pocket and the word was love.

The thought made her happy and sad at the same time. The letter hadn't mentioned her father. He was still a mystery. But at least she knew she had a mother who loved her.

Why had she abandoned her children? She thought of the dream she'd had so often over the years she was no longer sure if it was real or not. Was there a clue in the dream? Was that why it kept coming back to her in the quiet hours of the night?

She managed to find a spare seat on the train back. Sitting with her legs crossed at her ankles, she looked out the window but saw nothing. She was busy reliving the dream for the thousandth time.

She was a child, very young, too young to remember any of this. A fire was raging nearby. People were screaming. A man appeared above her, pushing her toward a door. A key was pushed into the lock. He had a thick Scottish accent. "Ahm awfa sorry it has tae be this way."

There was a thud and she looked up. The train had stopped. She was back in Leeds. How had that even happened?

She was home half an hour later. Before she even took her coat off she pulled out the key, crossing to the box which remained where she'd left it, teetering on top of the pile of books. "Let's see," she said out loud as she slid the key into the lock.

Holding her breath, she turned the key. There was a click deep inside the box and then the lid popped open.

What did that even mean? That her mother sent the box too?

She looked down. Inside was a single object.

A necklace.

A reddish pink oval stone on a thin gold chain. She lifted it from the box and then held it a couple of inches from her face. The almost pink stone became a deeper blood red in the light. Far inside was a black swirling smoke that seemed to move.

Was it from her mother? Had it once been hers?

She lifted the necklace over her head, glad of the length of the chain and the shortness of her hair. Once it was in place she pressed it to her heart. At once she heard drumming from nearby.

This isn't Jumanji. Where's that coming from? Has the tenant upstairs bought a drum kit?

The drumming grew louder. Instinctively she wrapped her hand tighter around the blood red stone.

One minute she was there. The next, she was gone. It was as if the necklace, and Rachel, had never existed at all.

Chapter Three

Cam was alone in his chamber. He was certain of that. Years of battle and intrigue had given him a sixth sense when it came to such things. He had been able to tell when Remigius the monk was hiding behind the curtain with the dagger waiting for him to fall asleep.

He had known that time in Castle Doune when the jester laid under the bed with the vial of hemlock ready to use. He had known when those two outlaws had concealed themselves in the sacristy while he talked to the bishop in Stirling only six months after becoming Laird.

He could tell when people were nearby. That was why he was certain there was no one in the room but him. That meant it was impossible that there could be a woman talking behind him.

Yet when he turned, there she was. Wearing the dark clothes of a witch, her hand clasped around a necklace. She stood by his bed, looking as shocked to see him as he felt to see her.

"How did ye get in here?" he asked, grabbing her by the arm. "Who sent ye? Answer me or feel my steel across your throat."

"Where am I?" she asked, seemingly oblivious to his threat. "Who are you?"

"You, witch. Answer me. Who sent you?"

"Where am I? What happened?"

A knock on his door. "My Laird, the people have gathered in the hall as you requested."

He cursed under his breath, dragging the witch over to the corner of the room. "I'll deal with you later," he said, opening the door to the garret and pushing her through. He slammed it shut on her bewildered face. That would hold her. The wood was hazel. It would counter any spells she might try and cast while he dealt with the gathering.

He locked the door, pocketing the key before turning and heading out to find Tor waiting for him, a nervous look on his face. He never looked nervous.

"What is it this time?"

"They are talking of leaving, my Laird. Of traveling south before it is too late."

"Curse them for a bunch of fishwives. Is this what the MacGregors are made of these days? Spines like eels the lot of them."

"Another castle has fallen. They say he is unstoppable. Some say he's the devil."

"Well, we'll have tae see about that, won't we? Come on, let's go nip this in the bud."

He put the witch out of his mind. She might have been able to sneak into his chamber without being detected but she would be able to do nothing else until he got back to deal with her.

First, he needed to deal with something much more important, the yellow streak that seemed to have begun infecting his clan.

He'd no idea where it had come from. In all the years of toil and struggle, not a man among them had ever suggested leaving their homelands.

"Someone is riling them up," he said to Tor as they descended the narrow stone stairs to the first floor of the keep. "I want to ken who is dripping poison in their ears."

"They're just scared," Tor replied. "Crivens, aren't you? Alice wants me tae take her south."

"Your own sister fears whispers that an undead King is sweeping the Highlands? Och, man. I thought better of ye than to be frighted by such nonsense. Or tae be swayed by your own kin."

"They're a simple folk, my Laird. As am I. I hold it important to shy my face away from darkness and trust in the Lord above all things."

"There is no mysterious barefoot man out there taking over the clans. There is only an ordinary man and an ordinary army and they can be defeated like any other. All this blether about the undead and evil forces is just what happens when there are gaps in knowledge, rumors fill in like rubble falling into a moat.

"We'll ken the truth when the patrols get back. We'll know who he is and where he is. Then we can raise our army in response and then we'll find out just how immortal this barefoot man is."

They had reached the bottom of the stairs by the time Cam finished talking. The noise of many voices talking echoed out from the great hall. Cam turned to face Tor. "Go find out who's been riling them up. They're good people and someone is taking advantage of them. I want to ken who and why."

"As you wish."

Tor headed to the outer staircase while Cam turned and headed for the curtain to the great hall. He paused to observe his Man-at-Arms heading away. He'd been in the post for the last three years and in that time had proved his worth in battle after battle. If he was getting scared, this was getting out of hand. It was time to take command.

Inside the great hall, four long tables had been laid out as at meal times, packed with more people than he thought the castle could hold.

More lined the walls. It felt as if the entire clan were there. The fires had not been lit. It was too early in the day. The air was warm nonetheless, the heat of so many bodies taking away any hint of chill. The conversation died as people noticed Cam's arrival among them.

Cam paused in the entrance, judging the mood of the room. Then he passed through the gap between the tables, heading for the dais, returning nods as he went.

He took his place alone in the great chair, leaning back and looking out at them all. They looked scared. He would have to handle things carefully. Yell at them and they would cower like children. Too conciliatory and they would run south like they threatened, thinking he was as scared as them, that he could not protect them.

He would protect them. They were his people. He'd been through too many wars to be scared of a single man, no matter how many rumors might swirl around him.

"MacGregors," he said, letting his voice carry across the room. "We are here today to discuss one thing and one thing alone. You all know what that is."

"Aye," said a couple of voices.

"The dark one," he heard a voice say. "The barefoot man."

He waved a hand and silence fell again. Eager eyes looked to him for guidance. He was their Laird, they needed to ken he had a handle on this.

He chose his words carefully. "I ken the rumors about land being swallowed by darkness from the Isles down toward us. I have heard tales of fish dying in the rivers, of crops failing, sunlight vanishing behind clouds and not returning. Look out the window. The sun still shines this day."

"The MacDougalls were starved out by January," someone shouted. "He is coming for us all. We should run while we still can."

"He kills bairns," someone else yelled. "Spikes the wee 'uns who did naeone nae wrong."

A mutter of agreement.

"We should sacrifice a virgin, appease the barefoot man before it is too late."

More agreement, this time louder.

"We cannot stay here." This voice shrill, panicky, coming from the back of the room.

Cam stood up, raising his voice over the hubbub. "I am your Laird and I will have silence while I speak."

The voices died down but the silence felt mutinous. He had never felt so out of control of his own clan. This was taking far more work than it had ever done before. Whoever was riling them up was doing a good job. It was all he could do to retain control over the mob.

"The patrols are due back any day. Until then, you must be patient and have faith in the strength of MacGregors, blessed by the Lord himself."

"What about the prophecy?" a voice shouted from the back of the room. "A sacrifice will save us."

"You ken as well as I ken that life is about the choices we make. No prophecy can overrule that."

"Your father believed in the prophecy."

"My father is dead and I am Laird now. He would have those who speak of running strung up by nightfall if they had not already died of shame for suggesting it. Let's hear nae more talk of running south. What do you think waits you down there in English arms? A warm welcome? To the north may be unknown but to the south is death most certain at the hands of the Normans. None will find shelter in that direction."

The door at the far end of the hall burst open and Tor appeared, shouting across to him. "They have caught a deserter, my Laird."

Cam pushed back his seat, crossing the room quickly. "We will continue this discussion later," he said to the clan as he went. He left them talking loudly as he followed Tor out to the courtyard.

"It was Martin," Tor said as they went. "Ran from the patrol. They got word to us just now from Wicke."

"I will deal with him at once. Any word of the rest of the patrol? What of Angus? It would take a dozen men to bring him down."

"He says they were all wiped out."

"A likely story. Get my horse ready."

"Already done."

"Then I shall see you soon, God willing."

They shook hands before Cam crossed to the stables where his horse was waiting.

Harry was standing proud, a huge black destrier none would dare try to ride except Cam. Straining against the stable-boys, four of them held him in place as Cam climbed onto his back. "Come on then," he said, "let's stretch our legs."

The stable-boys let go and then he was off, wind in his face as he rode out of the castle and headed rapidly north. Harry threw up great clods of earth behind them as together they made rapid progress to the village of Wicke.

They were there within an hour. Martin was being held in the blacksmith's cage. "That's not been needed since my father's days," Cam said to Martin as he brought his horse to a stop. "What did you think you were doing? You ken the penalty for deserting a patrol."

"Death is coming," Martin shrieked, his hands gripping the bars tightly. "It's coming for you all. You must run before it's too late."

"You will join me back to the castle," Cam replied. "You will face justice there and can make your case as you see fit."

Cam nodded to the blacksmith who unlocked

the cage. "Out you come," the blacksmith said, poking Martin with a long stick.

Martin looked warily around him as if he thought it might be a trap. Then he immediately took off, twisting away from the blacksmith's reaching arms, sprinting up the hill that led away from the village as if it were no hill at all.

Cam swore as he leaped back onto his horse, giving chase at once. Martin had no chance against a destrier yet he almost made it, running without pause until he reached the top of the hill, skidding to a halt at the edge of the crag.

The sheer escarpment looked down onto the icy cold loch far below. Martin stood on the very edge looking back at his Laird. "You have to run," he said, a note of pleading in his voice. "Before it's too late. He'll kill you all."

"Come back with me," Cam said. "I swear you will have fair trial before your peers."

"You dinnae understand," Martin said, his eyes wild. He was foaming at the mouth as he spat out the words. " You cannae stop him. He's no man at all. He's a demon."

"You know the law, Martin. You cannot desert a patrol. Let's have no more talk of ghosts or ghoulies that creep in the night."

"I will not go back," Martin said, shaking his head violently. He began to tremble as he spoke. "I've seen what he does to people. I willnae wait for that."

Without another word he turned and flung himself straight off the cliff edge. Cam could only watch as he fell from the sight.

The thing he remembered most afterward was that Martin never screamed. He fell in silence all the way down.

Back at the village, the people were gathered together by the cage. Cam found them all looking anxiously up at him. "Was it true?" one asked. "Is the barefoot man coming for us?"

"Martin was not in his right mind. Have no fear."

"Then where is he? What happened to him?"

"He chose to be judged by the Lord instead of his Laird. Half a gold piece will come the way of Wicke as reward for catching a deserter. You have my thanks."

He turned and headed back for the castle. There was nothing else he could do but wait for news of the northernmost patrol. He was not the superstitious type but even he could tell the omens were not good. Someone had appeared from nowhere just like the prophecy said.

No one knew his name but one clan after another had fallen to him as he worked his way slowly closer to MacGregor territory. He would get no further south, Cam would see to that. The rumors of him could be as wild as they liked. Rumors always swirled around the unknown.

In his father's day there were tales of a man from the Isles with one eye and the ability to fly over his enemies, burning them to ash with fire. He turned out to be a five foot tall bald sallow youth of no more than fifteen. One battle with the MacGregors and the fire breather was just one more corpse. Cam had no doubt this man was the same. A warrior who had fought well so far but a warrior nonetheless. One could be defeated in battle as any warrior could.

His thoughts dwelled on what would rumors could do to a man who let them take hold of his heart. They had made a man such as Martin desert. He had been a good fighter, a solid enough man in a scrap, though prone to a little too much mead when it was offered.

It happened sometimes, even without rumors. Perfectly good men just snapped. Often they refused to fight and next time a patrol went out they would find themselves quietly moved into laboring or the monastery. Only occasionally would they try to run from a patrol, and then justice would be applied, firmly, not harshly. Martin would have been sent to the monastery to atone for the rest of his life, his assets forfeited.

For him to choose death over that? Cam had never known anything like it before. Nor had the villagers. No wonder they were spooked.

He was still thinking when he arrived back at the castle. He left Harry with the stable-boys. Still deep in thought he walked out of the stable and across the courtyard, heading for his chamber to change, his riding clothes covered with mud of the road.

By his bed was a wardrobe. He picked fresh hose out, tossing it onto the bed before throwing off his baldric. As he went to lower his filth splattered hose he heard a hammering from inside the garret.

That was when he remembered the witch. It was a day without end, he felt, as he pulled the hose back up. He crossed to the door and listened carefully. There was the hammering again but it wasn't on the door. What was she up to in there?

He unlocked the garret quietly, pulling the door

open and looking inside. To his surprise she was over by the window, hammering the shutters back into place. The room was dark with the shutters closed while she worked on fixing them but his eyes quickly adjusted. He looked at her closely. She hadn't noticed him yet. He was just a shadow in the dark.

For a witch, she was a strange one. Her clothes that had seemed so witch-like at first looked different as he examined them a second time. She wore hose like a man yet different somehow. On her feet were black boots of a kind he had never seen before. She was so slender she looked like a strong breeze might blow her away. Her skin was pale, her hands almost dropping the hammer each time she struck a blow.

He was about to ask her what she thought she was doing when she pushed the shutters open. Daylight streamed in and all of a sudden she was illuminated like an angel. Her hair looked like it was on fire, golden shafts of sun piercing the dark curls, shooting out the other side, giving her a halo of light around her head. She turned away from the window with a smile that fell when she noticed Cam was right behind her.

He found himself wanting to look away,

ashamed of being caught staring secretly at her. He kept her gaze, making himself look her in the eye. What he wanted to say was gone.

She looked scared of him. So she should be. A click of his fingers and she'd be strung up in the courtyard, a warning to other witches. Could she cast a spell in time? He doubted it. She would have done so already. She was a fake like so many of them were.

"Tell me who sent you to kill me," he said, planting his feet apart and folding his arms. "And I better hear only the truth from your lips. I will ken if you're lying and it'll be the worse for you if you do. Now speak and speak well, your life depends on it."

Chapter Four

Rachel put the hammer down before answering. "You could start with nice to meet you." She held a hand out toward the hulking figure over by the door. "Anyone ever told you you're not the friendliest of hosts?"

He loomed over her, almost scraping his head on the ceiling as he snarled, "Speak, witch, or I will have you executed at once."

"I'm not a witch and if you were going to execute me, you'd have done it already. So why not just calm down and talk to me like a civilized person?"

She held her hands behind her back, hoping he couldn't tell they were shaking. She prayed she was

THE KEY IN THE LOCH

in the middle of a dream. If not, she'd just made the biggest mistake of her life.

He shook his fist in her face. "You will not bewitch me."

"Good to know. Now before this interrogation goes all searching spotlights and Nazi jackboots in my face, would you mind telling me where I am?"

"You are in Castle MacGregor and you are nae leaving until I get some answers."

"Castle MacGregor?" The name rang a bell but she couldn't think where from. Her head felt like she'd only just woken up from a very long sleep. She wasn't even sure why she'd fixed the shutters. It was just something she knew how to do, though she had no idea why. "In Scotland, right?"

The man took a step toward her. "Who are you?"

"The poor woman you locked away like this is some kind of fairytale. Got a dragon on guard downstairs?"

"Only the cook."

His expression hadn't changed but she was sure she saw a flicker in his eyes somewhere. "Was that a joke? I think that might have been a joke. You're not as unfriendly as you look." Maybe this dream was going to be more fun than she'd thought when he first locked her in.

"And you dinnae sound like any witch I've encountered before."

"That's because I'm not a witch. I'm a history student. My name's Rachel. What's yours?"

"Cam MacGregor, Laird of the MacGregor clan and the loch of ages, keeper of the keys, protector of the lands, warrior of all north of the Tay."

"I'll just call you Cam if that's all right?"

There was that flicker again. Was she amusing him or angering him? It was hard to tell.

"If you're nae a witch then who are you?"

"I just told you."

"That's no answer. What's someone with an English voice doing so far north and how did you get in my chamber without me hearing about it?"

She held out the necklace. "Your guess is as good as mine but I think it has something to do with this."

"What is that?"

"I touched this necklace and then next thing I knew I was here. I'm fairly certain this is a dream and, I realize I may not want to know the answer to this, but would you mind explaining why it looks like the Early Middle Ages out that window?"

"I dinnae ken what that is."

"No cellphones. No jeans. No tourists with cameras. If I didn't know any better I'd think I was on a movie set. It's weird."

He looked baffled, frowning as he crossed to the window and looked out. "I see nothing odd out there."

"Seriously?" She watched him as he leaned his head further out. It couldn't be much fun being so tall in a place with low ceilings. He had to bend his knees to get his shoulders low enough to look out properly.

He was wearing clothes that perfectly fitted the early twelfth century. She noticed that as she ran her eyes up his body, an idea forming in her mind, an idea she refused to contemplate. It wasn't possible. It was a dream.

"All is as it should be," he said, bending his body surprisingly nimbly to get back into the room. "Now the question is what am I to dae with you?"

"No, the question is what year is this?"

"The year of Our Lord eleven hundred and eighty-five."

"No, really. What year is it?"

"Eleven hundred and eighty-five."

A heavy ball thudded into the pit of Rachel's stomach. The thought that had whispered to her could be ignored no longer. "Really?" she asked in a faint whisper.

"Aye."

She reached out and prodded his chest, running her hand down toward his stomach. "You're real, aren't you?"

He took her hand and moved it to the wall. "As real as that stone."

"So this isn't a dream?"

He shook his head. "Nae dream."

"So I'm stuck in the past?" She fell back as if winded, staggering on her feet. She almost fell but Cam grabbed her, guiding her over to the only chair in the garret. He lowered her into it as she blinked up at him. She felt dizzy. It had to be a dream and yet he had felt so real.

"It's nae the past, lass."

"It isn't to you but it is to me. I'm telling you I'm from the future."

"That's more witch talk. Say nothing else or I'll run you through. I willnae have you casting a spell on me."

She opened her mouth to protest and then

closed it. She could show him the cellphone in her coat pocket, the couple of coins, her train ticket maybe. She thought better of it. He already thought she was a witch. Demonstrating a cellphone wouldn't exactly reduce his suspicion.

As her hand slid back out of her pocket, her coat fell open. He reached forward, grabbing hold of her necklace, examining the blood red stone closely. "Where did you get this?"

"It came in the mail. I think it's how I got here but look. See the smoke inside. It's not moving anymore. I don't know why but I think that's the key to this. Like the battery ran out or something. I reckon if I can get that smoke moving, I might be able to get back. Please, God, tell me I can get back."

"Mistress Abernathy has a necklace just like that. It's exactly the same."

"Who's Mistress Abernathy?"

"Runs the kitchens."

"Can I go see her? Maybe she knows something."

He shook his head. "They're twitchy enough without seeing an English witch in their midst. Go walking around there and even I'd be hard pressed to stop them from sacrificing you to appease the dark one."

"Human sacrifice? Great. What do we do instead then? You keep me up here like a pet for fifty years? If I don't get the necklace, there's no chance of me getting out of here."

"So if I get you the necklace, you leave without cursing any of the clan?"

"Exactly. Get me her necklace and I'm gone." She silently added a prayer that the necklace would work or else she'd just made a promise she would have no chance of keeping.

"Dinnae panic then. We just need tae wait until she's asleep."

"And then what? Tiptoe in like bank robbers and just lift it off her neck. You don't think she might mind?"

"She willnae ken. I can be quiet when needed. Why's the necklace so important tae ye anyway?"

She sighed. "This is going to sound crazy but I'm not from here."

"I ken that."

"Let me finish. I'm from the twenty-first century. This is the twelfth, right?"

"Aye." He sounded suspicious, like he thought

she was trying to trick him. "You're from the future."

"It's true. I know it sounds crazy but how else do you explain me just appearing in your room?"

"Casting a spell."

"I'm not a witch. I'm telling the truth. I traveled back in time and I get the feeling it was something to do with the smoke in the necklace. Now I've used it up and I'm stuck here. I can only hope your cook's necklace is still juiced up. Do you think you can get me the necklace?"

"Aye, maybe. If I choose to believe your story."

"There's an easy way to find out. Get me the necklace and watch me go. If I stay here, I'm a liar and you can do what you want with me."

"Prove you're from the future."

"What?"

"If you're from the future, prove it. What happens to Clan MacGregor? What happens tae me?"

"I don't know. I haven't got that far in the book yet."

"You're lying to me, trying tae bewitch me."

"I'm not. Look if I'm lying, why would I have this?" She reached into her pocket to pull out the cellphone when a voice reached them from the next room. "My Laird, are you in here?"

"Hold," Cam shouted before turning to Rachel. "Dinnae make a sound."

He crossed to the door and left. Rachel listened as he spoke to someone in the next room.

"The guards saw someone at the garret window, my Laird. Is all well?"

"I'm fine."

"I should check for intruders. Recall Remigius?"

"There's no need tae bother, I am alone."

"And I'm your Master-at-Arms, sworn to protect you. There could be an assassin in there at this very moment."

The door scraped back and then another Highlander was looking in at her. He was thinner than Cam, his skin wan like a candle. On his right cheek was a one inch scar that curled toward his eye as he smiled at Rachel. "Good day, lass."

"Hello," she said, returning his nod. "Erm, how are you?"

The man was already gone. She peered out to find him confronting Cam. "You said there was naebody there. Are you up to the same tricks as your father? You ken how that ended."

"Och, no," Cam replied. "This is my...betrothed."

"Really?" the other man said, his eyes narrowing. "And when did your bride-to-be arrive?"

"Since when do I have to explain my actions to my Master-at-Arms?"

His expression changed at once. The suspicion was gone. He looked as happy as could be. "Of course, my Laird. Apologies. I will tell the clan. What wondrous news." He clapped his hands together. "This calls for a celebration."

He was gone a moment later. Rachel stepped into the main bed chamber, scratching her forehead as she did so. "I might be wrong, and I probably am, but did you just tell that man I was your betrothed?"

"The truth would have you burned within an hour. What else could I call you?"

"A new servant?"

"He vets all the household staff. He'd have known I was lying."

"A cousin then."

Cam shook his head.

"Would that be so bad?"

"Aye, it would end with you getting killed when the truth came out."

"I thought a big tough Laird like you would be all alpha about such things. My way or the highway. Why not just run him through with your sword for his insolence?"

"You ever tried running a clan?"

"No but-"

"Violence only leads to more violence. I slay him, someone comes at me with a dagger in the night in revenge. He was brought into this clan as a result of marriage. Slay him and his father's clan wage war on us and I have enough problems. I am not my father. I have always ruled by law, not by fear." His voice lowered, as if he'd forgotten she was there. "And yet fear takes their hand once more. They talk of the need for sacrifice. We havenae done such a thing in more than a hundred years."

She looked at him. He was staring through her as if he no longer saw her. "What is it? There's something else."

"I dinnae ken why I'm telling you this but there's something up with them all. They're convinced the only way to make us safe is to sacrifice a virgin to the Old Gods. I will not go back to those heathen ways. We are a Christian people."

"So tell them sacrifices are out."

"They've been told but someone is stirring

THE KEY IN THE LOCH

them toward mutiny against my rule and I'm doing all I can to stem a rebellion. Until I find out who, how, and why they are like this, I need to be careful and you need to be my betrothed until you get yourself home again. Think what a strange woman walking about would do to them? You need to get back where you belong. Are you sure this necklace thing will work tae get ye away from here?"

"You believe me then?"

"Mebbe. Mebbe ah think you're a thief who wants the necklace to sell and I want to be there to see your story crumble around your ears."

A trumpet blew loudly in the courtyard, the sound echoing off the battlements. "What's that?" Rachel asked.

"The MacKenzies are here. Just what I need. You stay here and keep hidden."

"You're kidding right. I need to see this place. When am I going to get the chance to explore an actual medieval castle again? You have to let me explore it, at least for a little while."

He acted like he didn't hear her, walking over to the door and heading out to the staircase beyond. She heard a bolt scraping shut and then she was alone. She tried rattling the door but it was locked.

"Fantastic," she said, sitting on the edge of his bed and trying to decide what to do next.

There wasn't a huge amount she could do. She wasn't even sure if the cook's necklace would send her back to her own time. There was a logic to her idea but what was logic when a necklace had sent her hurtling back to medieval Scotland in the first place?

She stood up and looked out the narrow window. The Laird was down in the courtyard addressing a group of men on horseback, their tartan green in contrast to Cam's red. Even though they were above him looking down, somehow the power was still all with him.

She looked at his face as he talked.

It was a handsome face, she couldn't deny that. The dark glint in his eye, the sense of raw power barely kept in check by the few laws of the time.

His muscles outshone anyone she'd ever seen in the present day. He was clearly someone who had worked hard all his life, none of the courtly meals and piling on the pounds she would have expected of nobility of that era. He had deeply tanned skin from hours in the sun and hair that looked as impossible to tame as he was.

"Look mom," she said out loud. "I'm in a man's

bedroom. You'd be so proud. Betrothed to be married too. Haven't I done well?"

The bolt scraped back in the door and she turned in time to see the Man-at-Arms peering in at her. "The MacKenzies would like to meet the Laird's betrothed."

"He told them about me?"

"Would you accompany me down to the great hall?"

"Of course."

"This way, M'lady." The way he said it made her start but when she looked closer the smile was fixed on his face. He ushered her out the bedchamber and then down the flight of narrow stone stairs. Stepping out into a corridor she heard loud voices coming from behind a curtain.

"In here," he said, pulling back the curtain to reveal an archway that led straight into the great hall. Inside the conversation died at once as they all turned to look at her.

Two contradictory thoughts occurred to Rachel at once. The first spoke to the history geek inside her. She was seeing how a medieval feast was actually conducted with her own eyes. Talk about primary source material.

A fire burning in a brazier in the middle of the

room, ashes falling onto the stone floor below. Four tables all filled with rough looking Highlanders. Dogs curled up asleep on old rushes. The place smelled of men.

At the far end of the room was a dais and Cam sat at a lone table up there, looking out at her with barely concealed rage. She knew what that look meant. It meant she was supposed to stay out of sight.

At the same time as the academic in her drank in the details of what she saw another thought took over. It was fear.

None of the faces that had turned to examine her looked friendly. In fact a number of them looked more than a little bit threatening. She felt like Rapunzel walking into the tavern with Flynn Rider. Only there wouldn't be a song and dance number coming up. She'd be more likely to be sliced through before she took another step. Already swords were being drawn.

A huge figure burst into the room behind her, shoving her aside and marching past to dump an enormous tray of meat on the nearest table. "Out the way," the figure said, turning to glare at her on the way back. "I've enough to do without wee girls tripping me up."

Rachel caught a glimpse of a blood red necklace before the figure vanished.

Two men were on her before she had time to react. One pressed the tip of his sword to her chest before pulling it away. "You are real," he said. "I thought all this talk of Cam MacGregor marrying was but a fever dream. The man with no interest in women getting wed. Yet here you are. His betrothed, if you please."

"Hamish MacKenzie," Cam roared from the end of the room without getting up. "You would draw a sword on a MacGregor lass?"

"She's no MacGregor," Hamish replied, still looking at her, his sword hanging limply in the air. "I can tell that by looking at her."

"She will be a MacGregor when we wed and you will remain civil if you wish to get back to Castle MacKenzie with your head still on its shoulders.

"You cannot threaten me," Hamish snapped but his voice was already weakening. "We are bound by the oath of kinship between our clans."

"Hamish," another voice shouted in a voice that boomed around the walls. "Sit down."

"Yes, father," Hamish replied meekly, returning to his place at the table as the cook brought in trays of steaming vegetables with an army of helpers behind her.

Rachel looked for the voice that had shouted. It belonged to a man head and shoulders above those around him, and twice as wide as the nearest man. He examined Rachel with cold eyes before speaking again. "I would meet the woman Cam accepted in place of my daughter. You dinnae look like you're from here, lass. What clan claims you as its own?"

"The MacGregors," Cam said, marching across the room to take Rachel's hand in his. "Come," he said. "Sit with me."

As they walked past a sea of gawping faces, he leaned close and whispered. "Ah told ye to stay upstairs."

"Your man told me to come down."

"My man? What man?"

She took her place next to him on the dais looking out at a sea of murderous faces. She kept smiling at them all while whispering, "The one who found me, the one you were arguing with."

"Tor?" Cam sounded surprised. "I will deal with him later. Now you just play your part for now and we might might make it through this meal alive."

Chapter Five

Cam ate little. He watched the room, judging the mood of the place. It was ugly before Rachel made her appearance and it had only become worse since she'd joined him at the top table.

He had hoped to keep old MacKenzie from finding out about Rachel. Hubert had not forgotten or forgiven Cam for turning down his offer of Gertrude in return for half the acres north of the Wild Wood.

Cam told him in no uncertain terms that the time for talking of marriage would be in the future, once they had dealt with the threat coming from the north, the threat that at the time had been unidentified.

MacKenzie had been furious and only the growing threat to both of their clans had brought him to the table. He looked furious. Cam could understand that. Told that marriage was off the table and then finds out when he comes to parley that Cam is suddenly betrothed to this woman who's appeared from nowhere.

Why did he say betrothed? Why didn't he say something else? He shook his doubts away. It didn't matter. She'd be gone by the end of the day one way or another. If she was telling the truth she'd vanish back to her own time and would no longer be his problem.

What was much more likely than that nonsense story was that he would give her the necklace and she would try to run. He'd catch her at once and then he had two choices. Trial as a witch or give in to the clan's baser instincts and let them sacrifice her. Was she a virgin?

He looked at her as she ate, holding a chunk of meat in her dainty fingers. She had never borne children, he could tell that. Had she known a man in her time? It wasn't like the old days when you could be sure all those unmarried in the clan were pure.

The modern era had brought many changes,

one of which was an increasing preponderance for rumors to spread about women. He had heard several tales of girls either running away after suddenly becoming with child, or marrying when the bump was visible to all but the most blind.

He could do little about that, other than let God judge them when their time came. What he could do was find out about her. She had an honest face. A pretty one too the more he looked at her.

She ate softly, taking tiny bites and chewing for a long time, her skin pale as the whitewashed wall behind her. She looked like she hadn't eaten a decent meal for a long time. Picking up a cup, she took a slow drink.

"Is she a virgin?" Hubert asked.

Ale sprayed out from the goblet across the table. "Excuse me?" she asked, turning to look at him, coughing loudly as she did so. "What did you say?"

"Are you a virgin?"

She looked shocked by the question. "I don't think that's any of your business, thank you very much."

"So you're not then. No wonder your hair's uncovered. I might have guessed. Cam MacGregor would choose a harlot above my pure Gertrude."

Cam stiffened in his seat but before he could say

anything, Rachel spoke. "Actually, I am. Not that it should matter one bit."

He picked up an onion and bit into it. "It matters."

"Why? Can't marry someone who's been sullied, is that it? You're all right there. I haven't even been close to sullying. Sully and me live very far apart. Opposite sides of the globe in fact."

Cam had had enough. "We are not here to discuss my upcoming nuptials," he said, pushing his trencher away. "We are here to work together to fight the darkness that sweeps this land. Bickering will not solve that. Our enemy would be most gratified to know we sit here arguing this and that while he draws ever closer."

Hamish drained his goblet and then belched loudly. "We did not arrange a marriage in the midst of a war though did we?"

"Enough," Hubert snapped. "When is your patrol due back?"

"One of them deserted at Wicke," Hamish said, puffing his chest out proudly. "Cam had him tossed off the cliff rather than tell us what he saw."

Cam waited for the ripple of talk to die down. "Is this true?" Hubert called across to him.

"Once again your son takes gossip and turns it into fact."

"So you say there was no deserter?"

"One of my men did desert, that much is true."

"So where is he? What did he say of the bare-foot man?"

"Nothing. He threw himself off the cliff rather than return to face justice."

"Liar!" Hamish shouted. "You murdered him."

"Hamish," Hubert roared. "You will be silent for the rest of the meal or I will personally cram this goblet so far down your throat you will never speak again. Is that clear?"

Hamish went to open his mouth and Hubert raised an eyebrow. His mouth closed a second later and remained closed.

Cam nodded to the other clan chief before continuing. "The rest of the patrol are due back any day and we must be patient. Once we have the news they bring, only then can we discuss tactics. You are all welcome to stay here until they return."

"The virgin should be sacrificed."

"Who said that?" Cam asked, looking around the room. He looked in vain but the idea spread like a wave, growing stronger as each voice took up the cry. "Aye, a sacrifice."

"We must appease the Old Gods."

"The barefoot man cannot be fought."

"We must beg for their help."

"Sacrifice at midnight, like in the old days."

"Enough!" Cam shouted loud enough to quell them all. They looked at him but he saw what was in their eyes, especially when they looked at Rachel. He stood up and looked from one face to another. "The laws of the Highlands still apply. If a sacrifice was called for, the Laird would choose the one to be sacrificed. Last time I looked, I was Laird of this clan. There is no call for that barbaric practice anymore. Our enemy is a man and we fight him as men, not as heathens. I am in charge and there will be no more talk of sacrifice. If any of you wish to challenge me you do so now and you better make sure your sword is sharp."

He waited. No one said a word. "No? Then enjoy the meal we have provided in kinship and drink well. Where is the blasted cook? My goblet needs refilling."

He sat back down and tore off a hunk of meat from the chicken carcass in front of him. As he chewed his impatience grew. Where was the cook? She was embarrassing him in front of the MacKenzies.

"I will be back," he said to Rachel, getting to his feet.

"Please," she said, grabbing his arm. "Don't leave me with them. I don't trust them."

He tapped the top of her hand with his own. "Dinnae worry. You are under my protection. No harm will come to you. I swear it."

She nodded, letting go reluctantly. "I hope you're right."

"I'm Laird. I will protect you." He walked around the table and past the MacKenzies, pushing past the curtain and through the next one into the kitchen.

Mistress Abernathy's helpers were in the kitchen, sweat dripping off them in the heat of the roaring fire. "Where's Mistress Abernathy?" Cam asked. "Anyone seen her?"

Heads were shaken. No one had seen her since she'd brought the meat out a few minutes earlier. "We need more ale in there," he continued. "Someone take it in at once."

He passed through to the far door and out to the corridor beyond. The air changed. It wasn't just the drop in temperature from moving away from the kitchen fire. Something wasn't right.

He knew what had happened before he found

her. Down the stairs to the stores the sense of foreboding growing stronger with each step. He drew his sword. The lights had been extinguished. His eyes adjusted quickly and there she was. Her body had fallen in the middle of the room, her head resting too far back against one of the barrels in the corner. It looked as if the blow that killed her had been struck from behind. She'd staggered, one shoe coming loose. A pool of blood soaked the rushes below her head. He put a hand to her neck. Still warm. It had only just happened. Her necklace was missing.

He ran back up the stairs, sticking his head back into the kitchen. "Did anyone come through here but me?"

More head shaking. "None, my Laird," the spitboy said. "I would have seen them."

He cursed, ducking back into the corridor. The door to the courtyard that was usually kept locked hung open. He ran through it and into the open. Glancing around him, he saw plenty of people but no sign of whoever did this. It could have been any of them, he realized, feeling his grip on his people slip further. Who would kill the cook and why?

He marched over to the gate. "Shut it and keep it shut," he said to the guard. "Is that clear?"

"Yes, my Laird," the man replied, waving up to the tower above. The portcullis began to fall. Cam was already turning away, heading back to the keep. Tor was coming out from the great hall. "Hubert is asking what's taking so long."

"Mistress Abernathy is dead," Cam said.

"What? When?"

"Just now."

"But how?"

"I dinnae ken. Someone killed her, Tor. We need to shut the castle down until we find out who. No one in or out."

"Hubert's not going to be happy. He'll think it's a trap."

"He can think what he likes. For all I know, it was one of his men. No one leaves until we find out who killed her. Is that clear?"

"Yes, my Laird."

"Her necklace was taken. Find it and you find the killer."

"It will be done."

"Take my personal guard and get it done fast. I will keep the MacKenzies happy."

Tor rushed off to the armory to raise the guard while Cam headed back into the great hall. "What's this?" Hubert asked as he passed. "The portcullis has been lowered?"

He didn't miss a trick. Cam reasoned he must have someone watching the courtyard. He couldn't blame him. He'd have done the same. "I ask for your patience. There has been an incident and we are looking into it. I shall return shortly and you have my word that your freedom will be returned to you."

"Who are you to trap MacKenzies in your castle?"

"I have no time to bicker. If you wish to question my authority in my own castle, challenge me to fight this minute or hold your peace until I return."

He didn't wait for an answer, heading back out into the kitchen. Two of his guard were already questioning the servants. Good. He moved on, passing back down to the stores. Her body remained where he'd found it, Adam standing over her with his Bible in his hand. He turned when he heard Cam descending the stairs. "Tis an awfa business," Adam said. "I will pray for her soul."

"I thank you," Cam replied, kneeling beside her. "I will catch whoever did this to you," he said quietly, closing her eyes with the flat of his hand. He lifted her head, looking at the back of her skull.

"A single blow," he said, getting to his feet. "Whoever did this worked quickly. We heard nothing."

"Sound does not carry from down here," Adam replied. "I heard nothing until you were almost upon me."

"So she would not have heard them coming."

"Why would anyone kill her?"

"I do not know but her necklace has been taken."

"Folly. It will be recognized whenever they try to sell, the fools."

"Tend to her soul, Father."

"I will, my son. You tend to the living. Let me handle the dead."

Chapter Six

When Cam got back upstairs, he heard loud voices coming from the great hall. "Where is Cam?"

He passed back through the kitchen and into the hall. The place was in uproar. "We will not be held prisoner on suspicion of murder," Hubert said when he saw him. "You will release us or try us this minute."

"Who said anything of murder?"

"Your Man-at-Arms came in here and took your woman away. He told us everything."

Cam cursed silently. Tor had caused two problems for him already. Perhaps it was time to choose a new Man-at-Arms. Why couldn't he keep his mouth shut? "Where did he take her?"

"You look as if you're losing control of your clan, Cam MacGregor. Tell me again why we should look to you to lead us against the barefoot man?"

Cam didn't bother to answer. She'd be in the cell. He left the great hall, searching through his keychain for the one that led down to the pit prison. He didn't like the idea of her being down there. It would be all too easy for them to sacrifice a woman who couldn't escape, especially if they felt he was no longer in control.

Why did she have to come today? He had enough problems with the barefoot man and now the murder of his cook.

After unlocking the door, he almost crashed into Donald who was waiting on the other side. He pulled himself up short. "What have you done with her?"

"You told us to look for the necklace. She wears it brazenly around her neck. Tor showed me."

"Did he indeed? She already wore that, you fool. Release her at once."

"But my Laird."

"Now or you'll get my sword in your ribs."

"I do not have the key. Tor asked me to guard her."

"Out of my way." He shoved past Donald, ducking his head to avoid scraping it on the ceiling as he descended the stairs. At the bottom was a round room with an iron grill in the center. A heavy padlock sat at one end of the grill and he shoved his own key into the lock, looking down through the grill at Rachel who was curled up in the corner of the pit prison, lit only by the light of a single candle. Had she been beaten? He would have Tor's head on a spike if that was the case.

Pulling the grill up, he kicked the rope down and lowered himself down it hand over hand until he reached the floor. "Are you all right?" he asked, crossing to her.

She looked up, her eyes bloodshot. "They locked me in here. What am I supposed to have done?"

"They think you killed the cook."

"Me? But why?"

"You have the same necklace that was stolen from her."

"But that's stupid. I was wearing mine when she brought the food into the hall. Did they not consider that?"

"They did not consider at all. Come, I will get you out of here."

He held out a hand and she took it, getting slowly to her feet. "Did they hurt you?" he asked as he took hold of the rope once more.

"No, I'm all right."

"Good. Grab my waist."

"What?"

"Like this." He took her hands and wrapped them around him. Her face was an inch from his. "Hold on tight."

He began to climb, looking her in the eyes as he did so. The pit prison usually stank but all he could smell was the sweetness of her skin. He was glad when they were up out of the pit and he could stand away from her. "Come," he said. "You will stay in my tower tonight. I will keep you safe."

"But what about the necklace?"

"We will find it soon enough and get you home. You have my word."

"I don't mean that. How will you convince your men I didn't steal it?"

"Leave that to me."

He led the way through a maze of corridors, making sure to stay away from the great hall. Once they were up in his tower, he locked the door, something he had never felt the need to do before. With that done he turned to her. "You will sleep in the garret. I will put bedding in there for you. That way none will be able to reach you without getting through me first."

"Thank you. I am sorry."

"What for?"

"About the cook. I didn't say before and I should have done."

"It is done. What matters now is finding the killer before he strikes again. I sense dark hands in this and I dinnae like it. I must go back and deal with the MacKenzies. Will you be all right in here?"

"Could I possibly have some water?"

She held out her hands, blackened from the filth of the pit prison."

"Of course," he replied, unlocking his door and calling for a servant. Running feet echoed toward him and the spitboy appeared. "They are all busy. They sent me," he said, looking up eagerly. "What do you need?"

"Fetch me a ewer of water at once and a clean cloth."

"Of course."

The boy sprinted off. Cam stood by the door and waited, his hand on the hilt of his sword, ready to defend Rachel if the need arose. He would not have them sacrifice her, nor blame her for the death of the cook. They had been foolish to imprison her. She had been in the great hall when it happened. He would explain that to them soon enough and then they could get back on task, find the killer and bring them to justice.

The boy was back quick enough, splashing water from the ewer as he ran. He panted heavily as he brought the ewer into the room.

"Into the garret with it," Cam said.

Roger passed through the door in the far side of the room. When he came back he stopped dead, looking around him in wonder.

"What is it?" Rachel asked. "What's the matter?"

"I've never seen a room so grand," the boy replied.

"What's your name?"

"Roger, my lady."

"A good name. Here, you need this." She walked into the garret and came back with the dripping cloth. She wiped his face gently while Cam stood watching in wonder. What did she care about a spitboy?

"There," Rachel said. "There's a handsome young face under that grease." She looked up at

Cam. "You should treat your people better. He's just a boy."

"Och, he's a spitboy and paid well enough for his work."

"That's not the point. He's filthy."

"I dinnae mind," Roger said, squirming as she continued to wipe grime from his forehead. "I like grease. Means I can slip through the guards arms when they chase me." He grinned a toothy grin.

"Off you go," Rachel said. "I'll make sure he takes care of you."

"Thank you, my lady," Roger said, bowing so low his head brushed the floor. He turned and headed out the door.

"Boy," Cam said, beckoning him back. "Here." He reached into his pocket and pulled out a copper coin. "Don't waste it."

The boy's eyes widened as he took the coin. "Th…thank you," he said, sprinting off as if he feared Cam might snatch it back.

The Laird was just locking the door once more when he heard a scream behind him. He almost fell in his haste to get into the garret. How had they got to her in there? He barged the door open and was greeted by the sight of Rachel folding her arms across her naked chest.

"What's wrong?" he asked. "What happened?"

"Turn away," she said at the same time. "Now!"

He spun on the spot, facing the door and trying to wipe the image he'd just seen from his mind. The milky pale flesh, those slight globes of flesh and that perfectly flat stomach. He had caught the slightest glimpse before she made him turn around. He was certain the sight would stay with him forever.

He had no idea why. It wasn't like he'd never seen a naked woman before. The harlots in the towns that showed their wares when he visited, the peasants washing in the river, he'd seen plenty of bodies in his time.

"Do you always burst in on your guests?" she asked, the sound of rustling clothing reaching his ears.

"You screamed," he replied. "I was worried."

"You can turn around now," she said quietly.

She was standing with her coat tightly held across her chest. "Why did you scream?" he asked. "I thought someone had got in here."

"The water was colder than I thought. That's all. And it wasn't a scream, it was just a bit of a shock."

"You screamed."

"I did not."

There was a knock on the outer door of his chamber just as he went to reply. "To be continued anon," he said, leaving her in the garret. He closed the door to make sure she could not be seen before seeing who had knocked on his chamber.

"My Laird," Tor said, nodding when he saw him. "I thought you should know."

"Know what?"

"People are starting to talk."

"What about?"

"You and that woman. They say you are harboring a criminal, that she has bewitched you."

"Is that all?"

"The MacKenzies are threatening to burn down the portcullis if you do not let them leave."

"I will deal with them in a minute. First, tell me why you locked her up in the pit prison."

"It was not me. It was Donald."

"Either way, you locked up an innocent woman while the killer roams free. I should have your head for this."

"I am sorry, my Laird. I did not-"

A crashing sound echoed up the stairs toward them, drowning out Tor's words.

"Enough," Cam said, waving a dismissive hand.

"I will deal with the MacKenzies first before they destroy the place. Then we will discuss this further."

"Yes, my Laird."

Cam headed downstairs quickly, though he made sure to lock the door to his chamber first. He had plenty to worry about. A killer was on the loose. A rival clan was smashing up his great hall. A mysterious villain was sweeping across the highlands. Plenty to worry about indeed. And yet, as he descended the stairs, the thing he kept thinking about, was how the pale skin of Rachel's chest looked when he burst in on her, how it looked just like moonlight on the loch on a perfectly still night.

Chapter Seven

On the west side of Castle MacGregor there was a sheer wall of forty feet. It had been built over generations, the newer stone hewed into blocks that left no room for fingers to grip. No enemy could scale such walls during a siege. The lowest levels were older, darker stone, roughly cut, some mere boulders that had been heaved into place back when the castle was founded.

The MacGregors didn't care for the looks of the lowest levels of stone, hidden as they were behind thick undergrowth that had built up over many years. The higher levels were neater, smooth, imposing upon the surrounding countryside, stone that said we are here and we will not be moved.

At the base of the castle, thick briars and rose patches twisted and wove together, creating an impenetrable natural defense against attack. Pitch might burn it but in approaching, enemies would be stuck on the cruel inch long thorns, to be picked off by archers that trained every day to be sure never to miss their mark.

In the thickest patch of bramble, there was movement that night. While Rachel Fisher lay down for her first night's unsettled sleep, and Cam dreamed of the past in the room beside her, the castle guards paced along the battlements, looking out into the pitch black night for any sign of the barefooted man. One man alone was moving at the foot of the castle, making his escape.

Far below the guards, the brambles moved again. There was a rustling sound deep in the undergrowth and then a scrape as a door was forced open.

The door was hidden behind thick layers of ivy. Few denizens of the castle knew about it. One of those who did was forcing it open from inside, knowing that if he did not hurry, his absence would be marked, and from then on suspicion would grow about him. He had taken a risk shouting out in the hall that the virgin should be sacrificed just as he had taken a risk whispering in so many ears the tales of the barefoot man, undermining the Laird, sowing the seeds for what was to come.

He had not been careful for so long to throw it all away in one night. He had waited until the castle had settled for the night before making his move. If he had his way the meeting would have been arranged during the daytime, when he could have slipped out of the castle with the farmers and returned without arousing suspicion. Still, if he was back before light, all should be fine.

Most occupants slept together in the great hall, few of the inhabitants of the castle had their own chambers. It was not unusual for there to be coming and going as guards shifts ended and new ones began. The older clan members might be up three or four times in the night to visit the garderobe. Thus, no one thought it unusual when one more person got quietly to his feet and tiptoed past them, cloak wrapped around him to keep the chill out as he headed outside.

Once in the courtyard he had kept to the shadows, avoiding the eyes of the guards making their rounds. He held his hood close to his face, rehearsing what he would say if caught.

He needn't have worried. The guards were busy

watching for threats outside the castle. Word of a murderer in their midst had reached them all but they had bigger things to worry about during the dark. If they failed at their watch, the entire clan would be slaughtered. Their job was not to seek the killer in their midst. That job had fallen to Tor and he had yet to find any substantial clues to the identity of the killer.

The man in the hooded cloak made his way past the armory and into the stables. The horses stirred but the grooms slept on as he passed by like a whisper in the wind. The furthest stall was empty. It hadn't been used for decades, ever since the Laird's horse threw him and rumor grew that the stall was cursed. Grooms had heard strange noises coming from within, like bones creaking together when there was no wind to be heard outside.

Once inside the stall, the hooded man knelt down and lifted handfuls of old straw. Underneath were cracked flagstones that looked far more solid than they were. He curled his fingers under the central flag and, with a grunt of effort, lifted it into the air, laying it down quietly on top of the piled up straw.

Beneath the flagstone was the original floor of the stable. The solid rock surrounded a trapdoor that hadn't been used for a very long time. The hooded man pulled a key from his pocket. For a moment the moon appeared from behind a cloud and shone through the high stall window, catching the key in the light, flashing an intricately carved M that was marked into the metalwork.

With a turn of the key the trapdoor was unlocked. The man lowered himself through it, vanishing from sight.

He dropped to the ground with a splash, landing in the wettest and most ancient escape route of the entire castle, long forgotten by all but a select few. He was taking a risk that the old drainage tunnel would be discovered. He grimaced as the stinking water soaked through his boots. Glancing up, he looked at the open trapdoor.

If one of the grooms were to awaken and glance into the stall before he could return there was no hiding it. He would just have to hope the doctored ale he had provided them would ensure they slept deep and awoke none the wiser in the morn.

Ducking his head, he made his way through the tunnel in darkness, hands held out either side, brushing the damp walls to help him balance.

He passed a left turn, and then a right. He

ignored them both, moving forward until he reached the door at the end of the tunnel. With a shove he got it open enough to squeeze through into the undergrowth on the other side.

As quietly as he could, he eased his way through the brambles, catching his cloak on the wicked thorns several times and having to tear himself loose before he was out in the open. He paused, listening hard for any sound of the guards up on the battlements. No one was there.

The numbers of guards had been reduced by half, a large quantity needed to keep an eye on the MacKenzies who were not happy about having to spend the night there against their will.

It was touch and go for many hours whether things would descend into anarchy. That had only been avoided by two barrels of Cam's finest wine making its way out of the stores and down the necks of MacGregor's guests.

The liberal doling out of wine helped the hooded man. He had not touched a drop but the rest had, their sleep the sleep of the well soused. Many would pay with heavy heads the next morning but not him. He was far wiser, and about to become far richer.

When he was certain no one had seen him emerge he crept away.

It took two hours to get to the meeting place. When he arrived he wasn't sure if he was too late. There was no one there. The stunted oak was there, looking as ugly as ever. He walked around it twice before looking up at the sky, hoping the moon would emerge and help him work out the time. It remained hidden behind the clouds, the wind having died as he walked to the meeting.

He stopped, feeling certain someone was behind him. Spinning, his skin began to crawl. No one there. He turned again and leaning against the trunk was a man taller than him, his face also hidden behind a hood. His cloak did not reach the floor, it ended at his ankles, revealing a pair of bare feet that seemed to become part of the trunk of the tree, as if the man was there but not there. It had to be a trick of the light. They were just feet and he was just a man.

The hooded man who had crept out of the castle managed a half laugh, trying to cover his fear at being startled by the sudden appearance of the newcomer. "You gave me a fright, I thought you weren't coming. That I was too late or something."

The taller man leaning against the trunk said nothing, only lifting his hand up, palm out.

"Of course. I have it here." He reached under his cloak and brought out the necklace, passing it to the taller man. He noticed as he placed it on the outstretched palm, just how cold the man's skin felt. It was like touching ice. His hand remained frozen long after he withdrew it. "She's got one too, did you ken that? Of course you did, what am I saying? I might be able to get that one for you too if you like. What do you want it for anyway? No, you're right. It's no business of mine. You do what you like with it with my blessing. Just remember me when you take over."

The taller man looked down at the necklace for a moment before it vanished inside his cloak. When his hand came back out an instant later it held a leather coin-purse.

"Be ready," the taller man said, his voice like dust in the back of the throat, dry and hollow. "When the time comes-"

"Open the gate, I got it. Dinnae worry yourself. Castle MacGregor will belong to the barefoot man soon enough. Today the Highlands, tomorrow the world, am I right?"

The taller man was gone. The hooded man

looked for him but saw nothing. Almost at once he began to wonder if he'd done the right thing. Doubt gnawed at him as he walked back to the castle, doubt only assuaged by the weight of the coin-purse he carried at his side.

He was back at Castle MacGregor not long before daylight. He rushed back through the under-growth, catching his cloak on the brambles once again. After squeezing through the door, he pulled it closed, striding back through the tunnel and then up into the stable. A few minutes later it was as if the stall had never been entered. The flags and straw were back in place and he was taking his place amongst those in the great hall who were starting to stir.

He got up when the others did, stretching and yawning like them. No one suspected a thing. For all they knew, he had slept the night through with them, rather than taking the first step to joining a conqueror at his table. He grinned as he joined the others in line for the garderobe. Soon, he would not be queuing for anything. He would only have to snap his fingers and things would be brought to him for a change. He couldn't wait.

His smile faded when he caught sight of Mistress Abernathy's niece being comforted by a couple of the kitchen girls. She looked like she'd spent most of the night crying. It wasn't like it was his fault the girl had lost her aunt.

If the old bat had just handed over the necklace all the unpleasantness could have been avoided. She had to try and shout and then what choice did he have? He had to keep her quiet before anyone heard her.

He didn't think about what he would have done if she had handed the necklace over. She would have seen his face. She would have been able to tell Cam who had taken it even if she couldn't say why. He refused to think about the fact that there was no way she could have been left to talk.

It wouldn't matter soon. The coins had gone a long way to assuaging his guilt. What doubts he had would fade once the castle was taken. Then it would be him and the barefoot man ruling over the Highlands. Perhaps he might be granted Castle MacGregor for himself. What was the life of one old cook against ruling an entire clan? He would have killed far more people in return for becoming Laird.

Chapter Eight

R achel dreamed about the fire again. She was soaking wet. Why was that? She looked down. She was a child. Again? Why again?

She had always been a child. Her parents were outside the room talking in low voices. They often did that after she climbed into bed. She would fall asleep most nights listening to them talking about things she didn't understand.

Tonight was different though. Why was that?

They sounded different. They sounded scared.

The scream, a single long scream piercing the night from somewhere outside. That was when it all started to move too fast. More screams, the thunder of horses, and then the light coming through the shutters. An orange and yellow light that flickered and faded, snapping and crackling noises growing louder as the screams grew deafening. She sat bolt upright, her arms wrapped around her knees, too frightened to move. What was happening? Where were her mommy and daddy?

The door burst open and an enormous warrior burst in. His shadow cast a long line across the room. He had a sword by his side. Was he going to kill her?

He took a step toward her and she held her breath, too frightened to do anything. Then he walked straight past, stretching out with a key to unlock the cabinet next to her. It was a door that went into a tiny little wardrobe, a space that was barely big enough for a couple of sheepskin blankets that were only needed in winter.

"Where's mother and father?" her brother asked, sitting up in bed beside her, yawning loudly.

He grabbed her and her brother and shoved them through the doorway.

"What are you doing?" Alan asked, trying to fight him. "I want my daddy."

"Ahm awfa sorry it has tae be this way." It was the way he said it that frightened her the most though she couldn't work out why.

"I can't fit in there," she said as he pushed her in, the screams outside growing louder, the room getting hotter. Why was the room getting so hot all of a sudden?

"They will see ye again," he said, shoving them both through the door.

She winced, expecting to slam into the back wall of the wardrobe. Instead, there was nothing there but darkness. Her brother was beside her, clinging to her arm.

It was pitch black but something was breathing by her ear. It wasn't her brother, it was something else. Something bad was right behind her. It was there by her shoulder. If she turned to look at it, she knew it would grab her and drag her away. She was absolutely certain it would eat her alive. It reached out. Another second and it would touch her on the shoulder. Something brushed her side and she screamed. She glanced down and saw a pair of bare feet, adult, covered in dust, lit glowing red as if a flame burned within them. The feet belonged to someone she prayed would leave her and her brother alone.

A knock behind her.

The dream faded. Another knock.

She sat up in bed gradually realizing there was a

knocking on the garret door. It took a moment for her to remember where she was. The dream had been more vivid than ever before and she didn't want to forget it so soon. She wanted to immerse herself in it, try to make sense of the confusion that had been her constant companion for so many years. Who was she? It had more details that time, things she had never noticed before.

Another knock. This one louder accompanied by the rattling of keys.

"All right," she said. "I'm up."

The door opened and Cam stuck his head in. "Are you all right?"

"I'm fine. Why?"

"I heard screaming."

"Huh? Oh, I was having a bad dream. Hey. Did you lock me in here last night?"

"It was for your own safety."

"What if I needed the…you know?"

He frowned, not understanding.

"The bathroom."

"Ye are not dirty."

"Oh, good grief. What if I needed to pee."

He shrugged. "There is a chamber pot in the corner."

She looked and then looked back at him. "Well,

if it's all the same to you, I'll go use the toilet. Where is it?"

"The what?"

She sighed. It was too early in the morning to remember she was in the Middle Ages. "The garderobe," she said, rubbing her eyes as she climbed out of the bed. "And I don't suppose you have any clean pants for me to wear?" She shook her head before he could answer. "Of course not, medieval women didn't wear underwear."

"You can use the one in my chamber."

"I thought that was the Laird's use only."

He gave her a curt smile. "I say what goes in ma castle."

The smile was gone almost as soon as it came but while it was there it had lit up his face. Rachel squeezed past him out of the garret, feeling the heat of his body as he stood perfectly still. Once in his room there was only a door and curtain visible. The door led to the stairs so she headed to the curtain, pulling it back to reveal a long narrow passage that was plastered white. At the end she turned a corner and caught her first proper sight of a medieval toilet.

Sprigs of heather and rosemary were hung from the wall but no amount of herbs or dried flowers could mask the smell drifting up into the room. Holding her breath she glanced down through the wooden seat and immediately regretted it. The drop was sheer and ran all the way to the base of the castle.

Hoping the wood was solid, she sat shivering with the wind blowing up against her behind. Once she was done she looked in vain for toilet paper, finding only a pile of moss heaped on the seat beside her. It would have to do.

To her surprise it was softer than she expected. Feeling much in need of a bath or shower, she returned to the main bed chamber. "Did you have any luck last night?" she asked Cam's back.

He spun around from his position by the window. "Aboot whit?"

"Mistress Abernathy."

"Her killer is somewhere in the castle and we will find him. Her necklace is missing though. It seems that someone might know more about your idea for getting home than they're letting on."

"The necklace is gone? Then what are we supposed to do? I can't stay here. I need clean clothes. I need a shower. Oh boy, do I need a shower."

"You smell no bad to me."

"Don't I?"

He cleared his throat. "Ah have tae continue ma duties. You are to stay here until ah find the killer and the necklace. Then we'll see what's what."

"What about breakfast? I'm starving, aren't you?"

"We dinnae eat until noon here."

"Oh, right. I see."

There was a silence before someone knocked on the chamber door. "Stay back," Cam said, picking his sword up before pulling the door open. "What is it?"

"I brought the lass some fresh water."

Rachel peered out at Roger the spitboy, another ewer in his hand. "Oh, bless you," she said, beckoning him in. "Just what I needed."

He set the water on the table in the middle of the room before turning expectantly to Cam.

She looked at Cam and he looked from her to Roger before reaching into his pocket. "Ye willnae get a coin for every little thing ye do," he said. "Where did the last one go?"

"I gave it to mother. She said she can get me a wooden sword with some of it. I want to be a knight one day, just like you."

He began dancing around the room, fighting

off a dozen imaginary opponents. "Ye dinnae do it like that," Cam said after watching him for a minute. "Get your guard up. Here, hold this." He passed his sword to Roger. "Get your wrist around that way, that's better. Now, come at me."

Roger lunged. Cam neatly sidestepped, moving remarkably fast for someone his size. As he shifted, he stuck out a foot and Roger went sprawling to the ground. "Ye have a lot to learn," he said as he grabbed the sword from the boy. "You'd be killed if you fought like that in battle. Maybe you'd better stick to the spit."

Roger got to his feet, his bottom lip trembling. "Yes, my Laird." He scurried from the room.

"Hold up," Cam shouted after him, tossing a coin that Roger caught neatly. "Tell her to get you a shield too."

Roger beamed as he turned and ran off with the money. Rachel put a hand on Cam's shoulder. "That was a good thing you did just then. I can tell you like him."

"Och, that's nothing but blether," he replied. "Now, you stay here and I'll be back as soon as I can be."

Rachel lasted a couple of hours, not that she could track the time easily. She dared not switch her cellphone on. Who knew how long the battery would have to last before she got home to charge it again. When her stomach couldn't last any longer, she tried to distract herself but there was little in the bedroom to occupy her.

She was used to hunger gnawing at her from her teenage years but this was different. It was hunger mixed with anxiety. What if the necklace didn't turn up? What if she could never get home again? What was she supposed to do?

Another hour or so went by and still there was no sign of Cam. Her stomach growled but she tried to ignore it. She leaned out of the window and caught sight of Roger far below in the courtyard. He was waving a wooden sword at a chicken that continued to peck at the mud without taking the slightest notice of him.

"Roger," she called out, waving down to him.

In return his sword waved back and he beamed up at her. "I'm going to be Laird of my own castle someday," he shouted back.

There was a gruff laugh from the blacksmith passing him by. "That'll be the day," he added.

Roger looked crestfallen. "Don't listen to him," Rachel shouted. "You'll make a great Laird."

His grin returned. "You really think so?"

The door creaked open behind Rachel. She turned. "You've been a long-" Her sentence cut off. It wasn't Cam standing there, it was three surly looking denizens of the castle.

"I told you," one of them said, nudging the man next to her. "Look what your Laird has landed for himself!"

"Look at what?" Rachel asked, backing slowly away from them as they approached her. "What are you pointing at?"

"Where'd you get that necklace?" the woman asked.

"It's mine."

"Likely story. You stole it when you killed the cook, didn't you? You're a witch. Come on, admit it. You've addled Cam's mind. Why else would he keep us MacKenzie's here? You want a war between us, don't you?"

Two of the men reached out and grabbed her, holding her in place as the woman grew nearer. She reached out, pulling the necklace from Rachel's neck. "Was it worth it? Murdering an innocent woman?"

"I didn't kill anyone. Let go of me." She fought to free herself but they had too tight a hold of her.

"Come on. We'll take her back with us."

"Where are you taking me?"

They began dragging her toward the door. One of the men sneered at her. "We're going to sacrifice you to the barefoot man. Save us all before it's too late."

"No time for talking," the woman replied. "Quick, before he finds out."

A voice from the stairway beyond the door. "He's already found out."

Cam moved so fast, by the time Rachel worked out what was happening it was over. Cam had flashed his sword so close to her face she felt the wind whip by her.

Her three attackers were no longer holding her. They were all on the floor, blood pooling under them, their bodies perfectly still. Cam's sword dripped as he stood over them, waiting to see if any of them moved again.

"What just happened?" she asked, staggering backward. "Did you just kill them?"

"Are you all right?" he asked, dropping his sword and placing his hands on her shoulders.

She couldn't help herself. She threw her arms around him, closing her eyes tightly. "I want to go home," she said quietly.

"I know," he replied. "You will soon enough."

"You killed them," she said, realizing she was pressed against him. She could hear his heart through his chest. It was steady, calm, unlike her. "I can't believe you killed them."

"They were going to murder you," he replied. "I heard them talking as I was coming upstairs." He nudged the nearest one with his foot. "Now to try and explain to Hubert why I killed three of his clan."

As he spoke, a trumpet rang out in the courtyard, stopped, then rang again. "What's that?" Rachel asked.

"The patrols are back."

Chapter Nine

Cam's mood darkened as he listened to one tale after another. He had sent out three separate patrols to ascertain the truth of the barefoot man's assault on the Highlands. The patrols had come back as one for protection, something that they'd never done before. Safety in numbers was the only reason they were alive.

He sat in the great hall on his dais. Hubert sat beside him as a mark of respect between the two clans. Cam had decided to wait until after the patrols had finished their reports before telling him about the death of three of his own.

He had left her in his chamber with three guards

outside. He wasn't risking anything happening to her again. It felt as if control was slipping away from his fingers. In all the wars and intrigues of the Highlands it had never been like this. Perhaps there was some truth in the rumors that the barefoot man was demonic. How else could he explain a murder in his own castle, the killer still roaming free somewhere?

Angus was talking. He was a grizzled man of more than fifty and Cam looked at him closely. He had never seen fear in Angus's eyes but it was definitely there. He stood stock still, a long ugly looking scar on his right cheek. "They came upon us in the night. We heard nothing, my Laird."

"Go on," Cam said, glancing across at Hubert to see the old man also showing a flicker of fear.

"They took out half a dozen of us before we knew what was happening. Martin ran while we were fighting. I have not seen him since."

"Martin has been dealt with. Did you see the barefoot man?"

"We saw no one. They were little more than shadows. Once we started to gain the upper hand they simply melted away."

"What of the Western Isles?"

Angus shook his head. "The darkness has

spread to them, my Laird. Half are empty, the rest belong to him now."

Cam swore under his breath, gripping the edge of the table.

Hubert coughed loudly. "How is it even possible that so many strong clans can fall to one man?"

Angus turned to him. "The few survivors we found all tell the same tale. He attacks as he did with our patrol. He comes in the night, attacking again and again, wearing them down. There is little to fight against. By the time they muster armies he has vanished and when they sally forth, he either swallows them up and they are not seen again or he takes the castle while they hunt for him and then they are besieging him. It is attrition that he craves. They say he enjoys seeing the carnage more than anything."

"Then that is it," Hubert replied. "We must move south while we still have room to maneuver."

"Never," Cam replied. "This is our home. He is a man like any other and I say what I have said before. He can be defeated."

"You heard him," Hubert said, looking wild eyed. "The prophecy is coming true. The barefoot man will swallow the Highlands for sport."

"Sacrifice," Hamish said from the end of the

table. "That will save us. I have already given the orders, Father."

Cam stood up, turning to face Hamish directly. "My sword is still stained with the blood of the last of your clan who tried to take my betrothed for burning. Would you attempt another assault?"

The color drained from Hamish's face. "They do not have her?"

Hubert turned to his son. "What are you talking about? What have you done this time, Hamish?"

"I did it to save us all, Father."

"Did what?"

Cam waved at Angus to sit down before turning to Hubert. "He sent three of your people to my chamber to take my betrothed. They were to burn her to appease the barefoot man."

"And where are they now?"

"They lay staining my floor with their blood."

"You would kill MacKenzies while we parley under a flag of truce?"

Hubert was on his feet too, his hand going for his sword. "Why should I not run you through right now?"

Cam did not stir. He looked at the old man and his sword. That fire was still in his belly even as his body aged and began to fail him. "What would you do if MacGregors came for your wife?"

"Run them through."

"Then you do not dispute my right to protect my betrothed?"

Hamish scoffed. "You cannot take his side, Father. Give him his way and all the Highlands will fall just like the prophecy foretold."

Hubert slid his sword back home before sinking into his seat. "I am too old for this. I say we travel south to safety. What say you, Cam MacGregor? Will you accompany us? Remember what Angus said? Safety in numbers."

"I say we hear the reports full through. Then we eat. After that I will have an answer for you."

Angus got back to his feet. "We sought him everywhere but those castles that belong to him rained arrows upon us if we came within a quarter of a mile. We have no tale from those on his side, only those who fled the slaughter of their clans. The MacDonalds are gone, the MacDougalls are with him. The Frazers hold out to the east but the rumor is he heads that way after taking our lands, the MacKenzies too."

"What do they say of him? Has anyone seen him?"

"Some say he's a demon, others a necromancer. Some talk of him as a druid who uncovered the secret of alchemy. They say that is why he moves so swift, the armor of his army is silent, the weapons unbreakable."

"We'll see about that," Cam replied. "Go on."

"That is all I hear, my Laird."

"No description of him?"

"Only that he travels barefoot and cloaked. He has no weapon himself, only his voice which is enough to kill, so I am told."

"You have done well, Angus. Get that wound tended to and then get some food inside you. What about you, Philip? How did you get on?"

All heads turned to the corner of the room where a white haired man emerged from the shadow. The MacKenzies muttered amongst themselves. No one had seen him there. Cam had to resist smiling. He could have slit Hubert's throat from his hiding place before he even knew what was happening.

"You saw me, my Laird," Philip said. "Your eyes grow keener."

"And you are as loud as a pig on a frozen lake."

Philip smiled. "I would talk to you alone, my Laird."

"Very well. Tor, ensure our guests are as well fed as the patrols. I will be back presently."

He stood up, the room standing as he swept past them and out into the corridor. "This way," Philip said. "The walls have ears."

Cam followed his old sword master out of the great hall and across the courtyard to the chapel. Once inside, Philip locked the door and then the shutters, leaving the two of them illuminated by only the light of a single candle upon the altar. "I hear you have a woman in your chambers," Philip said, his voice low. "A woman who does not belong here."

"Who told you that?"

"The entire castle knows. Do you remember what I told you in the burning forest?"

"That one day my fate would be decided by a woman. How could I forget?"

"She is that woman."

"Och, that's nonsense. She's…"

"She's what? Beautiful? Entrancing?"

"Odd."

"So are you, my Laird, if you do not listen very carefully."

Philip leaned back against the wall, motioning for Cam to sit. He did so, feeling himself a child again, an odd feeling for a Laird. It was like the old days, Philip talking to him, telling him things that no patrol could ever find out. He was silent on his travels, discovering things he had no right to know but whenever he came back, it was to impart knowledge to the Laird in waiting, knowledge that had kept Cam alive when many other Lairds had fallen in the clan wars.

"Darkness sweeps the Highlands," Philip began. "And there is only one way to end darkness."

"Dinnae tell me you want me to run with the MacKenzies."

"Och, no. You confront darkness with light. The woman is the light. Take her north."

"I will not sacrifice her."

"That is not what I ask. She seeks Mistress Abernathy's necklace, does she not?"

"Aye. Why do you care?"

"The necklace has gone north. You must take her after it if you are to save the clan."

"You cannae be serious. I must stay here and defend the clan. Why build a castle if I am to abandon it when it is most needed?"

"I tell you not what makes sense. I tell you only what must be done. You must go north and you must go at once. Already you may be too late. Any more delay will be fatal to us all."

"I hear what you say, Philip, but I cannae do it. I cannae abandon my people."

"Then we are all doomed." Philip headed for the door, sliding the bolt back and turning his head as he did so. "I thought I had trained you better than this."

"You trained me to think for myself and that is what I'm doing."

"As you say, my Laird."

Philip stepped outside. By the time Cam was in the open, he'd vanished. "I wish he wouldn't do that," Cam said out loud as he returned to the great hall. He glanced up as he walked, sensing he was being watched. From his bedchamber window he saw Rachel looking down at him. He waved up at her and she returned the gesture.

Why did he care so much what happened to her? It wasn't just the prophecy. He felt a connection to her, strange when he had known her for such a short spell. Was she a witch? A thief? A traveler through time as she insisted? He could not say what was the truth about her. Perhaps she was all those things, perhaps none of them. She was pretty, there was no denying that. He thought once again of how she'd looked when he burst in on her washing. The paleness of her skin. From nowhere he wondered how soft her skin was, what it would feel like to run his hands along it, to press his fingers into her lower back, draw her toward him, their faces coming together, her breath on his cheek.

He marched into the keep, shaking the thoughts away. This was not the time to swallow a love potion. It was a time for action.

The occupants of the hall rose to their feet as he entered. "Have you made up your mind?" Hubert asked.

"What about the murder of our people?" Hamish shouted.

Hubert turned to his son. "You hush your lips my boy if you wish for them to remain attached to your face. Understand?"

Cam walked to his seat before speaking. He took a deep breath and looked out at the anxious faces waiting to hear what he had to say.

"If you wish to go south," he said to Hubert. "I will send a body of men to protect you but the MacGregors remain here. If we be the only beacon of light in infinite darkness, we will remain. And if the barefoot man is a demon, if he swallows us whole, we will be assured of a seat at the high table of the Laird of us all. I say we will have greater chance of success if the MacKenzies and MacGregors come together here. What say you to that, Hubert MacKenzie?"

Hubert pressed his hands together as if in supplication. "We will die if we remain here."

"Where is your backbone?"

"Where was your desire for harmony between our clans when you rejected my daughter's hand in marriage?"

"Now is not the time to discuss that, Hubert. We have bigger matters to attend to."

"Now is the time. You are betrothed to that trollop in your chamber. What clan is she even from?"

Cam clenched his fists, his knuckles turning white as he resisted rising to the bait. "She is a MacGregor."

"She is a Sassenach and you would bind your future to the English over a true blooded Scottish clan?"

"If you fear the barefoot man, that is your right. You need not be ashamed of fear."

"I am not afraid of anything."

"Then why do you run south?"

Hamish was up fast but Cam was faster, his

sword out and held high to block the blow of the MacKenzie boy. "Are you certain this is how you want to die?" he asked as he pushed Hamish backward. "Is this the hill you want your life to end upon?"

"I will not die here," Hamish spat. "You will." He raised his sword and brought it down hard.

Cam ducked back and the sword wedged itself in the chair where he had been sitting moments before. Hamish tugged at it but it would not come free.

Cam looked about him. The MacKenzies were already up, locked in battle with the MacGregors. "She must be sacrificed," Hamish screamed. "Someone go get her from his chamber."

Cam looked at his men. They could fend for themselves well enough. He was more concerned about the half dozen MacKenzies slipping out of the great hall. He ran after them, his sword drawn.

"Psst," a voice said to his left. He glanced that way and saw Philip beckoning him from the end of the corridor.

"I have no time," he said, already running.

"Cam," a female voice hissed. He looked again and Rachel was with Philip, her worried face peering from the corner.

He skidded to a halt, running down that way and finding her waiting out of sight from the MacKenzies.

"Are you all right?" he asked, grabbing her hands. "Did they hurt you?"

She shook her head. "I'm fine."

"I left three armed men guarding you," he said. "How did you get out of there and down here without them noticing?"

"I got her," Philip said.

"I might have guessed."

"Dinnae worry so. It looks like your hand has been forced, does it not?"

"Take her somewhere safe, I can handle the MacKenzies."

Philip shook his head. "Tor and I will deal with them. You get her north and find that necklace. It is the only thing that can bring an end to this conflict."

"Try not to kill all the MacKenzies."

Philip smiled. "Take her through the sally port and travel to MacIntyre Castle. The necklace is in the treasury. They managed to get hold of it during a skirmish. Be careful, he may have taken the castle since I was there."

"How do you even know where the necklace is?" Rachel asked.

There was a crash and the sound of running feet from around the corner. "Go!" Philip said.

Cam looked but he had already vanished. He did not fancy the MacKenzies chances. "Come on," he said, grabbing Rachel's hand and running the other way. "Time to move."

Chapter Ten

There were two guards at the entrance to MacIntyre Castle. They had been on shift since nightfall and were not going to be relieved until morning. Both were exhausted. Knowing that their territory was shrinking did not help with the stress of their work.

At any moment they might be attacked but nothing had happened for weeks. Guarding was dull work at the best of times and their shifts had lengthened as more patrols were being sent out to try and regain their lost territory.

One of the guards yawned loudly.

"How's your bairn?" Jock asked. "Ready to wield a sword yet?"

"Hardly. He's teething and it's all Mary can do to get him to sleep at all."

A voice hissed out from above. "Keep your voices down."

They glanced up, seeing the Sergeant at Arms glaring at them from out of the window above. They nodded and he vanished. Jock continued, his voice lower than before. "He's worse than usual."

"Wouldn't you be?"

"Do you think he's real then?"

"Who?"

"You know, the barefoot man."

"I dinnae ken about that. All I ken is I need tae take a pish. You all right on your own?"

"Aye but dinnae let him see you away from your post. He won't spare you the lash this time."

"Och, I'll only be two minutes."

Jock stood alone, gripping his pike and staring into the darkness. There was a twig snap to his left, James no doubt.

Out of the blackness of a night a figure emerged, shuffling along the track up to the castle. "Is that you, James?" he asked.

The figure came closer. It wasn't his colleague, it was a beggar, and a leprous looking one at that. His hand was the only thing visible under his cloak, hanging limply, the skin looking wan in the flickering light of the torch on the wall by the portcullis. Boils covered the back of his hand.

"Stay where you are," Jock said. "We want no diseases spreading in here."

"What diseases?" the man said, lifting his hand into the air.

Jock frowned. How had he thought the skin diseased? It looked as healthy as his own. "What do you want?" he asked.

"To come inside and warm myself is all. It is a cold night."

"None admitted until morning, Laird's orders.

The man pulled back his hood, revealing a bald head. "Do you know who I am?" the man asked.

"A beggar who'll get nothing from me but a boot up his arse."

"Look again," the man said, nodding down toward the ground. Jock looked down, seeing the beggar's bare feet. Fear rose up in him as he slowly looked up once more, seeing the man smiling and nodding. "You do know who I am. Or should I say, you ken who I am? I am in Scotland after all."

"Please," Jock said. "I have a family."

"How nice. I, unfortunately, have not been blessed in that way yet. There is still time though in the future. Now, I would love to stand here and talk with you all night but business must intrude for a spell. Are you going to unlock that door so I can walk in like a civilized person?"

"I cannae do it. The Laird would kill me."

"And I'll kill you if you don't let me in. Do you see the pickle in which you find yourself?"

"You have no weapon. How will you do it?"

"I won't do a thing. I will not harm a tiny little hair on your Scottish head."

Jock straightened up, feeling bolder. "Then be on your way, kind sir."

"Last chance."

From his left there was a muffled scream. It died as soon as it emerged. It was followed by a heavy thud. "What was that?" Jock asked, panic bubbling up in him.

"That was James," the barefooted man replied.

"I thought you said you wouldn't hurt us."

"No," the man said, his smile fading. "You misunderstood. I said I wouldn't harm a hair on your head. A knife in the guts is much more effective. Or perhaps I'll take out your eyes." He clicked his fingers.

At once the torch died. The entrance to the castle was plunged into darkness. Jock swung his pike and jabbed at empty air. He nearly screamed when a voice whispered in his ear. "What's it to be. Let us in or die?"

"I can't."

"Oh, but you can," the voice whispered even closer. "There is a knife in your ribs this instant. You turn and unlock the door and I will let you live. You can even join us, if you wish."

"I can't. I dinnae have a key. They unlock it from inside in the morning."

"Well isn't that a shame," the voice whispered. "If only you had a key." He clicked his finger again and screams began to ring out from inside the castle.

"What was that?" Jock asked. "What are you doing?"

"You said you had a family," the man said, pushing the knife slowly forward. It moved through Jock's armor as if it were moving through butter. "Dinnae worry, lad. They will join you soon enough."

Jock slumped onto his back, looking up at the castle walls above him. Lights were going out up there. The screams he heard began to grow louder. When the torches were relit a few minutes later all Jock saw was darkness. He heard nothing at all.

The barefoot man flicked his hood back over his head as the portcullis was raised, the door behind sliding slowly open. His men stood behind it, awaiting his command. "Are they all dead?" he asked.

"Stacked in the pit prison to a man."

"Was she among them?"

No one spoke.

"Well?"

My Lord," one said, shuffling on the spot. "We could not find her."

"Don't look so afraid," the barefoot man said. "Come, walk with me out here a moment."

The man followed him out into the darkness, as unable to resist as if he had been told to stop breathing. "I am sorry, my Lord. They have not seen her. Perhaps she remains at MacGregor Castle. Or maybe she's gone onto Tallis already."

"Perhaps she has."

A minute later the barefooted man walked into the castle calling for ale. The man who had told him of their failure did not join them in the castle. His body slid slowly down into the moat, sinking below the surface, vanishing from sight.

Chapter Eleven

MacIntyre Castle lay thirty miles to the northwest from MacGregor Castle. Rachel knew that from her guide to Scottish castles. She found it surreal that the ruins she knew from her research were no longer ruins. They were homes, filled with people, all of them with lives as rich as her own.

Roger, the spitboy. Would he grow to become the Laird that he wanted to be? He had survived early childhood so he had a good chance. In an era with 50% infant mortality, he had done well just to make it this far.

She found herself thinking about the inhabitants of MacGregor castle as they traveled. Cam had said little during the journey. Whenever she looked across at him, his brow was furrowed. There was no doubt he was lost in thought.

The first night they had rested in a small glen surrounded by wizened trees. If fairies had darted out in the darkness she would not have been surprised. It was that kind of place.

Lying in the darkness, she had felt afraid and cold. She was certain Cam was already asleep, his breathing slow and steady as she lay shivering, trying to settle on the heather underneath her, the scent of it filling her nostrils.

Then out of nowhere his arm had wrapped around her and he'd drawn her body against his, being the big spoon to her little. She thought she'd object but she didn't. At once she felt safer.

Not only that but his body seemed to burn with an intense heat that warmed her better than any fire could ever do. With his chest pressing into her back, she closed her eyes, saying nothing.

She fell asleep feeling his breath on her cheek but when she awoke he was nowhere to be seen. She sat up at once, starting to panic. It was one thing to be lost in the Middle Ages with a strong Highland Laird at her side, it was another entirely to be lost and alone without even a clue which way she was meant to be going.

She shouted, "Cam," at the top of her voice and he came running into view over the top of the glen.

"What is it?" he asked, weaving between the trees to reach her. "What's wrong?"

"I thought you'd left me. I thought I was all alone."

"Och, I'd gone to fetch breakfast. Here." He passed her a couple of purple carrots.

"You know," she said, gnawing on the end of the larger one. "These are orange in my time."

"Orange?"

"It takes some getting used to, being here."

He grunted, biting his carrot in half and swallowing it at once.

"You'll get indigestion if you eat like that."

He was already on his feet. "Come on, we have a long way to travel today."

"Will we get there by tonight?"

"I dinnae ken but there's no chance if you dinnae get up."

For the first hour he answered her questions, explaining what had happened the previous night in the great hall. As the morning went on, his answers became shorter until he only grunted in response to her questions. Eventually she gave up, lapsing into silence and concentrating on the walk.

Her feet were starting to give her trouble. The shoes that had been perfectly suitable for her adoptive mother's funeral what felt like a lifetime ago were no longer handling things as well.

They hadn't been designed for route marches through the Highlands of Scotland, especially when the trails were little more than rabbit tracks through thick grass and heather.

She had no doubt that by the time they stopped, her feet would be red and raw. She hoped they would find the necklace at MacIntyre Castle and she could get home, soak her feet in a hot bath before lying on a comfortable bed that had a roof over it.

She suddenly felt a strange sense of loss. What was that? She was supposed to be looking forward to going home. What was that pang deep inside her? Probably just hunger.

It would be strange to go home after everything she'd seen. She'd seen people killed. That wasn't something she was likely to forget in a hurry. She'd been the only twenty-first century person ever to get to see what a Medieval castle was actually like to live in. Wait until she started her Masters, she'd be able to describe exactly how things were all those years ago.

She glanced at Cam as he walked a few feet in front of her. His back was perfectly straight, his legs swinging as if he'd only walked a few yards, not miles and miles on no more than a couple of carrots. What was he thinking about?

She wished she could remember more of her studies. Then she'd know what happened to his clan. She certainly couldn't remember anything in her books about a barefoot man taking over half of Scotland, claiming one castle after another. But then, there were gaps in the histories. Would Cam be defeated? Would his castle fall like the rest?

It seemed impossible that anyone could defeat him. The speed with which he'd moved when she was attacked was incredible. He had felled three people in seconds. It didn't seem possible that he could be killed. He certainly didn't look worried.

They stopped in the late afternoon. Rachel was glad of the rest, her feet were killing her. They sat on a hilltop above a cool clear loch. The only sound was that of an eagle soaring far above them.

There was no wind, the sun warm enough for Rachel to remove her coat and lay back on the soft heather, closing her eyes while she kicked off her shoes.

"Why did you not tell me?" Cam asked.

She sat up on her elbows and looked up at him. "Tell you what?"

"The state of your feet. They're bleeding through your hose."

She looked down. He was right. "I thought they were just blisters."

"You should've said. Wait there."

He moved away, his eyes scanning the ground. She watched as he squatted down and ripped something from the earth. Returning to her, his fists moved together, mashing green leaves smaller. He spat into his hands, continuing to grind the mixture. "Here," he said. "Get your hose off."

She slid her socks down, wincing as the fabric brushed past the bleeding patches. The pain was worse in the open air and it was all she could do not to cry out. She didn't want to, not with him glaring at her like that.

"Keep still," he said, kneeling at her feet and pressing the mixture to her right foot. At once the pain died, a warmth moving up her legs as he rubbed the poultice gently over her skin. She watched as he moved to her other foot.

He was a confusing sight. His face suggested he was furious with her and yet his hands moved softly, causing no pain at all. His enormous fingers were surprisingly nimble, administering the last of the mixture before he sat back on his haunches.

"Dinnae touch it. Get your hose over the top and it should protect ye for the rest of the day. I'll put more on tonight. Now come, we need to get moving again. Time is against us."

"Can we not rest a little longer?"

"I dinnae ken what is happening back at home. I dare not tarry."

Whatever he had applied to her feet made a huge difference. Not only had the pain gone when she began to walk, her energy level improved. The rest of the day passed pleasantly enough. Without thinking about her feet she was free to let her mind wander as she looked at the changing scenery around her.

What she noticed most was how quiet it was. That day they passed a couple of traders with carts but no one else. No cars racing past along the road, no sirens in the distance, no airplanes in the sky. Just the birds circling the mountaintops and the leaves rustling in the breeze whenever they passed a copse of trees.

It was just growing dark when they reached their destination. The first Rachel knew of it was when they crested a hilltop and there in the valley was a dark mass of stone, towers at four corners. Cam stopped dead, staring down at the castle.

"What is it?" Rachel asked.

"I dinnae ken," he replied, "but stay near me. I dinnae like this. It's too quiet."

She could see what he meant. There was no sign of life anywhere around the castle. From her time with the MacGregors she was used to seeing people continually passing in and out of the gates, farmers on their way back to their fields, traders, children, fishermen, all the life of a clan in full flow.

There was none of that here. MacIntyre Castle was a desolate place. "Were they attacked?" she asked as they descended the rocky slope toward the castle entrance.

"There is no sign of battle," he replied, drawing his sword and holding it by his side. "No guards on the door neither."

"Do we have to go in? I've got a bad feeling about this place."

"The necklace is inside. We must go in."

They reached the door which hung open on its hinges. Cam went first. "Keep behind me," he said, shielding her with his body. He walked through the archway into the courtyard which was as empty as outside.

"Where is everyone?" Rachel asked.

He didn't answer, moving quickly across to the keep. "The treasury is at the bottom of these stairs," he said. "I remember it from last time I was here. Come on, let's get this over with."

Into the keep, he headed down the stairs, stopping at the bottom. "This isnae good," he said when he reached a solid wooden door barely visible in the gloom. "It isnae locked." He pushed it open and looked in. "Empty."

Rachel waited while he searched. He emerged looking angrier than before. "It's been turned over. Come, there is nothing for us here."

"But how am I supposed to get home?"

"We will have to work something out. For now, let's get gone. There is only death here."

As if the castle itself were answering, from somewhere in the distance, a moaning call echoed, softly at first, but then louder.

"What was that?" Rachel asked, grabbing Cam's arm.

"We shall see," he replied. "Let me listen." The moaning grew louder still. "That's coming from the pit prison."

Chapter Twelve

❦

Cam pushed past her, up the stairs and along the corridor deeper into the keep. By the time she caught up with him he was already descending more stairs, and then more.

At the bottom were other open doors and Rachel had to stop. The smell was overpowering. Holding her nose, she tried not to gag as she followed him down.

In the blackness at the bottom she dared not go any further. A spark flashed and then she saw what was happening. Cam was using a flint to light a candle he'd found.

Once it was lit, the dim yellow glow illuminated a small room with a trapdoor in the floor by Cam's feet.

"What is that smell?" she asked.

"Dinnae look," he replied, kneeling as he peered through the trapdoor. "You dinnae need to see this."

"I'm not a child," she replied, kneeling beside him and almost throwing up at the sight. Through the trapdoor she could see the pit prison. Bodies had been thrown in, their limbs tangled together, jutting out with fingers pointing accusingly upward, as if to blame the two of them for their fate.

"Look," Cam said, squinting in the dark. "There."

Rachel nearly screamed. Part of the mass of corpses was moving. She was about to scramble away when she realized what it was. Someone was alive in there. Fingers were moving.

"Get me a rope," Cam snapped. "Quickly."

Glad of the chance to move away from the hideous sight, she searched in the gloom, finding a length of rope beside a broken barrel. It was attached to an iron bar in the wall, presumably for lowering food to those in the pit prison. Cam took it from her, his eyes still fixed on the moving arm he could see.

He put his sword on the ground before tying the rope around his waist, lowering himself through the open trapdoor. "Be careful," she said, tapping him on the shoulder as he descended through the gap.

"Be ready," he replied. "You might need tae run."

She watched in silence as he landed on the pile, reaching down and grabbing the protruding hand.

"Haud on," he said, pulling with all his strength. Slowly a person emerged from the mass of bodies. It was an elderly man, dried blood coating his face, his eyes tightly shut.

His white hair was matted with filth and as Cam helped lift him through the trapdoor, she saw his eyes were still shut. Why didn't he open them?

She hauled him up, using all her strength until he was finally onto the floor beside the trapdoor. Cam clambered up the taut rope before untying the knot around his waist, kneeling beside the prone figure. "What happened here?" he asked. "Can you hear me?"

"The barefoot man," the man said, his voice faint. "His men took my eyes. He came in the darkness. I saw him by the light of the moon, directing his men. They killed them all. They laughed while they did it. Then they threw me in there with the rest.

"I was only here to sell my pig. What did I do to

deserve such an awful fate? I felt sure I would starve in there until you saved me. God bless you both."

"Where is he now? Where did he go?"

"I dinnae ken. Please, get me some water. I beg you."

"Come on," Cam said, hauling the man to his feet. "Walk with us."

The man shuffled, stumbling many times before they got him out into the courtyard. "Is my home safe?" he asked as they emerged into the night. "My wife? Is she alive?"

"Where do you live?"

"The farm's the other side of Glen Currie Tower. Five miles north of here."

"We'll take you there."

"Och, you're good hearted people. Bless you both."

"Do you ken what happened to the treasury?"

"Aye. He took it all. Said he was going to dump the lot in Glen Currie Tower while he sallies forth."

"Then we must go there."

"No," the man said, grabbing Cam by the shoulders. "You must leave it be. Seek the treasure out and you'll be slaughtered like all these people. He knows no mercy, none at all."

"Let's get you back to your wife, then we can

talk about what to do next." He turned to Rachel, mouthing the word, "necklace."

She nodded in response.

They left the castle, the blind man leading the way. "I ken these roads well enough," he said by way of explanation. "You should go back south. I can make my own way home. You've done enough."

"We will get you home," Cam replied. "It willnae take long."

"Then what will you do?"

"That's our business."

"No offence, I'm sure. There should be a fork coming up. We need to go left."

Rachel was glad to put the castle behind them. The place smelled of death and the aura stuck to her for a long time before gradually ebbing away. She couldn't stop thinking about the bodies, about so many lives wiped out for no good reason, just because one greedy man wanted all of Scotland to himself.

The tower on top of Glen Currie was only visible when the moon emerged from behind clouds. The old man was for giving it a wide berth but Cam took them straight along the road toward it, ignoring his protests. "Wait here," he said when they reached it. "I shall be but a moment."

"Dinnae go in there," the old man said. "Death awaits you if you do."

"Och, dinnae talk soft," Cam replied. "There is no one for miles around but us."

He tried the door. It was unlocked. "Inside," he said. "Where I can keep you both safe."

The old man tried to protest but it fell on deaf ears. In the end he allowed himself to be guided into the tower and up a flight of spiral stairs, emerging into a small room crammed full of scrolls and bottles. Some were neatly aligned on shelves but others had fallen onto the floor.

"I see no treasure," Cam said. "I think you were misled."

"On the contrary," the old man said. "I see all the treasures of the world right here."

Rachel looked at him. He was standing taller, blinking as he opened his eyes to stare at them both. The wig slipped from his head, revealing a bald dome criss-crossed with scars. "I've waited a long time to see you again, Rachel."

"What? Who are you?"

Cam had his sword drawn in under a second, swinging toward the man who neatly stepped behind Rachel. Cam only managed to divert the blow at the last second, almost catching Rachel on top of her head.

The man grabbed Rachel, holding her in front of him. "You smell good," he said, sniffing loudly and taking a step back from Cam. "Put the sword down, my Laird."

"You're him, aren't you?" Cam asked. "The barefoot man."

"So they call me. And your clan will not save this girl for a second time. She's going to help me, aren't you my dear?"

"Get away from me," Rachel said, trying to squirm free from his inhumanly strong grip on her arms.

He gave her a shove. "Go on then," he said with a sneer. "Off you both go."

They looked at him and then at each other. "Oh," he added, looking like he was barely suppressing a laugh. "Before you do, perhaps you'd like one last look at this." He reached into his tunic and brought out a necklace. Rachel recognized it at once. It was identical to her own.

"Where did you get that?" Cam asked.

"Are you that foolish?" the man replied. "Now Rachel, this is between you and me. Take my hand

and the two of us go back to your time. What do you say?"

"If you know what the necklace does, why wait until now to use it?" she asked, waiting for the right moment to snatch it from his grip.

He shook his head. "I need you. Don't you see? You're the key. Now, come. Take my hand and we can rule the world together."

"Never," she replied. "I'd rather stay here and die than let you get your claws in my time."

"You're under the impression you have a choice," the man said with a smile. "I don't need you alive to do it. I just need your hand."

He reached into his tunic again, this time bringing out a dagger. He threw it through the air. Cam stepped in front of Rachel, lifting his sword in front of his chest. The dagger hit the hilt and flew off to the side.

The old man swore out loud. "Cam MacGregor. Join my side and I will grant you all the lands from your castle to the Northernmost Isles. A handsomer offer you could get nowhere else."

"I do not do deals with demons," Cam replied.

"Last chance or I kill you both." He grabbed a bottle from the shelf beside him and hurled it to the floor. Green smoke began to rise from it. "One lungful and you're dead," he said. "Make your mind up fast."

There was a creak above his head. In the time it took him to glance upward the ceiling developed an alarming crack. "What the-" he began before there was a crashing sound and the entire ceiling fell in, someone falling through it and landing on him.

Cam grabbed Rachel's hand, running for the stairs. They were down in seconds, bursting out in the open a moment later, both gasping for air. Cam turned at the sound of footsteps, his sword ready. "I will not let him hurt you," he said.

"Good to hear," a voice replied.

Rachel looked at the doorway in time to see a figure emerge. It was the man who'd fallen on their attacker. "Who are you?" she asked.

The man shrugged. "Just a common or garden thief. Who are you two?"

"I am Cam MacGregor, Laird of my clan. This is Rachel Fisher and she is under my protection. You shall not harm her."

"I have no intention of harming either of you. I just wondered if you wanted to buy a necklace?"

He held out the necklace the barefoot man had been holding. Rachel smiled and Cam let out a laugh. "You stole that from him?"

The man shrugged again. "I was happily seeing what to steal when you lot turned up. Hiding in that ceiling wasn't comfortable. Neither was falling through it. Before I knew what was happening he'd gone out the window and you two were out the door. He went so fast he left the necklace behind. I thought I deserved something for my trouble and you seemed mightily enamored with this little thing. What's it worth to you anyway?"

"Give it to me and I dinnae run you through." He had his sword to the thief's throat a second later.

"I want a bit more than that."

"A place in my army with hot food in your belly everyday. I could use someone like you."

"Sounds good enough to me." The thief tossed it to Rachel. "Bit aggressive, your mate, isn't he?"

Rachel frowned. "Aren't you bothered that you could have died in there?"

"I could die any day of the week. So could you. Our slippery friend upstairs on the other hand…" He shuddered.

"You know who he is?"

"Let's just say if I knew it was his tower, I wouldn't have been trying to steal from it."

"Did you see which way he ran?"

"You will not catch him now. He'll be back with his people."

"How do you know?"

"I know a bit about that one. I even know how he can be defeated and I'd be happy to share that little tidbit for the right price."

Cam reached into his money-belt and brought out a coin, tossing it to the thief. "This better be worth it."

"There's a woman locked up on Kirrin Island. She holds the key to his demise."

"That's it?"

"That's all I found out. I'm a thief, not a seer. I only overhear things from time to time. You want him dead, go see her. Goodnight all."

He was gone in seconds, disappearing into the darkness, leaving the two of them alone.

"Put it on," Cam said, turning to Rachel.

She stared down at the necklace. How had she come to the past? She'd put the necklace on and grasped it in her fist. Logically, doing the same would send her back to her own time. "What are you going to do now?" she asked.

"Go to Kirrin Island and see what I can find."

"Alone?"

He nodded.

"You'd do better with a second pair of eyes."

"You're not staying. You need to get home where it's safe."

"And you might be a Laird but you're not the boss of me."

"This way," he said suddenly, grabbing her hand and sprinting away from the tower.

"What. What is it?"

"People," he replied, glancing behind him. "Lots of people."

Chapter Thirteen

C am stopped running an hour later. Carrying Rachel over his shoulders reminded him of his early training. He set her down in a dark valley far from Glen Currie Tower.

"How are you not even out of breath?" Rachel asked, looking at him as he stood looking back the way they'd come.

"I spent years training with a tree trunk on my shoulders," he replied.

"Are you saying I'm like a tree trunk?"

"No, lass. You're a lot lighter."

She looked past him. "Are we safe?"

"For now."

"What do we do now?"

"You put the necklace on and go home."

She shook her head. "Not until I find out what's on the island."

"Why? Why not go now while you can?"

"I don't know." She sank to the ground, sitting cross legged and leaning back on a tree stump. "Something tells me I need to stay with you for a while." She shivered. "Anyway, can we make a fire?"

"I dare not. They would see the glow. Come, sit beside me."

He held out an arm, wrapping it around her as she shuffled across to him. She felt safer and warmer at once. "Is that them?" She could just hear movement in the distance, the sound of twigs snapping and muffled voices talking low.

"Aye but they are going the wrong way. I left a false trail for them to follow."

"Should we get moving?"

"Not yet. We would make too much noise. We rest here until I am sure we are safe to go on."

"To the island?"

"Aye."

She shuffled closer to him as a cold breeze blew past. "How do you know where it is?"

"Kirrin Island? I went to the monastery there to be blessed when I came of age. It was some time ago but I remember the route well."

"How long will it take?"

"We will reach it tomorrow, God willing. You should try and get some sleep while you can."

"I doubt I'll ever sleep again." Her stomach rumbled loudly in the darkness.

"You are hungry?"

"I'm fine."

"Wait there." He got up, heading away. He didn't want to leave her but he couldn't let her starve. He went back the way they'd come, searching for the rabbit warren he'd seen a few minutes earlier. He found it and it didn't take long for him to trap two of the more foolish ones. He brought them back to her.

"We go on," he said. "Down there is a sheltered spot. No one will see a fire no matter how hard they look."

A few minutes later they were in a sheltered glen next to a loch. Cam soon had a fire going and the smell of cooking meat filled the night air.

"Tell me something," he said, looking at Rachel in the darkness. "Why aren't you going home now?"

She shrugged. "I told you. I need to stay."

"To see what's on the island?"

"Exactly. I'll tell you something though, when I do go home, I'm going to have quite a few stories to tell."

"What about?"

"About here. About you, about this time."

"It's different to your time then?"

"Oh, like you wouldn't believe."

"Tell me about it."

"What do you want to know?"

"I dinnae ken. Tell me about your necklace."

"What about it?"

"How did you find out its powers?" He leaned forward to turn the makeshift spit. The rabbits dripped onto the fire, making it hiss loudly.

"I didn't. It just happened. It came in the mail. I mean a messenger brought it to me in a locked box."

"How did you get in the box?"

"I found the key after the funeral."

"Whose funeral?"

"My mother's. Well, not my mother, my adoptive mother. I was at her house after the funeral when I found a box from my real mom. It had a tartan blanket in it just like that tartan you wear."

"Like this?"

"Yep. That and a key with an M on it. The key opened the box. The box had the necklace in. I put it on and then bang, I'm here with you."

"I'm sorry about your mother."

"I didn't get on with her."

"I didnae get on with my mother either. Didn't stop me hurting when I saw her head on a spike."

Rachel looked up suddenly. "Sorry, back up. Your mom's head was on a spike?"

"Aye, both my parents. There was a siege. We would have been all right if it wasn't for the fire. They burned their way in then got them both. I barely escaped with my life. For months I had to see their heads on spikes before my people retook the castle and freed us."

He pushed the memory away, having no desire to relive it. The fire racing through the village outside the castle walls, the scream of his mother as she was torn from him. He picked up the rabbits, letting them cool for a moment before slicing meat from one and tossing it to Rachel.

"Eat," he said, chewing his own food slowly.

"I'm sorry about your parents," she said quietly.

"It's in the past," he replied. "Now, eat, then we must sleep while we can."

He stamped out the fire, settling down on his side by the embers, once more wrapping around Rachel to help keep her warm as the night drew on. She was soon asleep and he couldn't help but breathe in her scent. It helped distract him from thoughts of the past.

The next morning he was up early, feeling groggy. Several times in the night he had to comfort Rachel. Ever since he'd met her she seemed plagued by nightmares, moaning and shifting in her sleep. She awoke a while after him, sitting up in time to see him returning from fishing.

After they'd eaten, they moved on. It took most of the day to reach Tallis on the shore of Loch Kirrin. The loch itself was close enough to the sea to have tidal currents and the island could not be swum to, the current itself too strong.

"That is Tallis," Cam said as they stood looking down upon the village on the shore of the loch. "The people are still there at least."

"Why has he not attacked them?"

"Perhaps because this place is so well hidden. Or perhaps because it has always been a sacred place. God might protect them from harm. Let us hope He does the same for us."

They walked down the slope to the village, passing by onlookers who stopped to stare at them as they went forward. By the time they reached the middle of the village a large crowd had grown.

From it emerged the village elder who Cam recognized from the time of his blessing.

"Will," he said, holding out a hand. "You've grown more rotund since last time I saw you."

The old man shook warmly. "And you've grown into a man who should know better than to mock an elder."

The two of them laughed, Will slapping Cam on the back. "What brings you here?"

"We need to get to Kirrin Island."

Will's smile faded. "There's nothing out there for you."

"Nonetheless, we need to get there."

"I see. Then you better come with me, you and your friend."

The crowd parted to let them through. "Have you heard of the barefoot man?" Cam asked as they walked down to the boathouse on the shore.

"Aye," Will replied. "I've heard tales of him."

"Do you not fear him?"

Will shook his head. "Come, you have time to break bread with me before you row out there. You will find no food on the island."

"We will be fine."

"Would you deny an old man his request?"

Cam sighed. "Very well, but make it quick."

They turned from the boathouse and up the street to a large two story stone house. Will stopped in front of it, pulling the door open. "After you."

Cam let Rachel go first, following her in. There was another door creating a porch. He followed her through that. The door slammed shut behind them. He turned, trying to push it open again but it was firmly bolted in place.

"What are you doing?" he asked, shouting through the wood.

"I'm awfa sorry," Will replied. "He only let us be if we swore to lock up any who tried to cross to the island."

"You are in league with him?" Cam slammed his fist into the door.

"Save your strength. I will have food brought to you while we await his arrival."

Cam turned to Rachel. "You have time. Take the necklace. Save yourself."

"You don't get rid of me that easily. Is there another way out?"

They examined the inside of the house but it

had been effectively turned into a prison. The windows were barred, the walls nothing but stone. All objects had been removed. There was nothing they could do but wait.

Cam peered out of the window that faced the shore. The island was visible in the distance. They were so close and yet so far from it. "What if the thief was lying?" he asked. "What if he only said that to get us here?"

"Why give me the necklace then?" Rachel countered. "I think I can get us out of here. When they bring the food, let me do the talking. Okay?"

Cam nodded. "What will you do?"

There was a scrape at the door and they turned in time to see it opening. A guard stood there. "Against the back wall," he said, not moving.

Cam and Rachel did as he asked, leaning against the wall as he brought in a loaf of bread and a jug of ale. He set them on the floor and turned to go without another word.

"Hold on," Rachel said, pulling a black object from her pocket. "If you do not release us, I shall trap your soul in this."

The guard frowned. Cam tried to see what she was holding but could not work it out. The object beeped and then lit up. "What is that?" Cam asked.

Rachel ignored him, pointing the thing at the guard while pressing something on the box. She turned it to face the guard and he cried out, falling to his knees. "Please," he begged, shuffling toward her. "Let my soul free."

"You will let us out of here at once."

"Anything, please."

"Cam, tie him up."

Cam did as she said, taking the guards cloak from him and using it to bind his limbs, tying tight knots as he continued to stare at the box in Rachel's hands.

Only when he was bound, with a length of cloth as a gag, did she press the box again. The light faded from it.

"Your soul is safe from harm," she said to the guard who nodded frantic thanks.

"What is that thing?" Cam asked, looking at the box as she slid it away again.

"It's called a cellphone."

"And what did you do? Did you trap his soul?"

She crossed to the door and pulled it open. "I took his photo."

"Photo? What's a photo?"

"I'd show you but the battery's nearly dead. I

wonder what I would have done if I'd had some signal."

"You're making no sense."

"I'll explain when we're somewhere a bit safer. Now how do we get out to the island?"

He peered out of the door. "We get down to the boathouse and row across. Move quickly and we should be all right. They're all over there in a big group. Looks like the barefoot man is here. We better be swift."

"No doubt they're getting ready to welcome the barefoot man."

"No doubt. Come, let's go."

Cam led the way, taking Rachel's hand in his as he walked swiftly across the road and down to the boathouse. Inside were four rowing boats. As Rachel climbed into the end one, Cam thrust his sword through the wood of the remaining three, leaving rapidly filling holes before he joined her.

Taking the oars, he pushed off and began to row. As he did so the door to the boathouse burst open and the barefoot man appeared, sprinting down to try and grab them.

He didn't make it.

With his hand outstretched too far, he fell into

the water as Cam rowed ever faster, the boat cutting through the water toward Kirrin Island.

"Enjoy your exile," the barefoot man shouted after them, the villagers pulling him from the water back to safety. "I will come see you soon enough."

Chapter Fourteen

R achel couldn't explain to Cam why she chose to stay. She couldn't really explain it to herself. She had the necklace in her pocket. At any moment she could put all this behind her.

She looked back at the village of Tallis, shrinking away behind them as Cam rowed steadily toward Kirrin Island. The villagers lined the shore, looking out at them. Behind them the great bulk of Glen Currie, the tower invisible in the cloud that swirled around the mountaintop.

The weather had turned, the sun disappearing as if in control of the barefooted man. Rain began to spit down and she wrapped her coat closer around her, thinking how soon she could be at home. She could have a bath, get some clean clothes on, brush her hair for the first time in days. It must look awful.

A cold wind blew, attempting to push them sideways. Cam fought against it, his muscles bulging as he worked the oars.

Did he not feel cold? There he was bare-chested except for his tartan baldric. She sat facing him as he rowed, looking from him to the island behind. He stared at her unblinking, rhythmically working the oars again and again.

She thought, not for the first time, how handsome he looked. Was that why she hadn't gone yet?

She could admit to herself that she would miss him. It wasn't something she would ever say out loud. How would it sound telling him she was staying to spend a little longer with him?

Once she went home, she doubted she'd ever get a second chance. This was it. Only if she had no other choice would she use the necklace. She needed to go with him to the island even if she didn't know why.

What did he think about her? It was impossible to tell. There were times she wished she was more normal and this was one of those times. She wished she understood body language better. Did he like her?

He was keeping her warm at night, he was looking after her. But was that something any man would do? Or something he would do for any woman?

He had given her no signs about whether he liked her or not. Or he'd given the signs but she'd not noticed them. She sighed to herself. Her head was starting to hurt from thinking about it.

"Do you think we'll be safe on the island?" she asked.

"We'll find out soon enough," he replied. "Tell me what that thing was in your pocket."

"This?" she replied, pulling out her cellphone. "I'm just glad it worked."

"What does it do?"

"It lets me talk to other people that have one of these."

"How?"

"I'm not sure. I'm no engineer. I know it sends signals out through the air and they get received at the other end. That's about the best way I can describe it."

"Can you show me?"

She shook her head. "There's no one else in this time with one of these."

"Can you show me how it traps souls."

"It didn't trap that man's soul. I just took a picture of him."

Cam frowned, not understanding.

"Like a portrait, a painting but faster."

"With no brush? Show me."

"The battery's almost dead and I'm not sure when I might need to use it again. I promise I'll show you before I go home though."

"Deal. How far?"

She looked past him toward the approaching island. "Not long."

"Then I better get moving. Who knows if he's found another boat to come after us."

Another ten minutes passed before they reached the shore. Cam brought the boat to rest on an old jetty, the wood rotten, several planks missing.

"Watch your step," he said, helping her out.

She wanted his hand to remain on top of hers, feeling a pang of loss when he pulled away. What was it about him that made her feel safe every single time he touched her?

"How big is this place?" she asked when they

stepped off the end of the jetty onto the rough grass that covered all the land she could see.

"Not too big. There's the monastery and a couple of old fishermen's cottages. If the woman is here that the thief spoke of, we'll find her soon enough.

"Which way?"

"We'll try the cottages first."

She followed him across the grass inland to the far side of the island. It took about an hour to reach the far side, the terrain growing tougher the further they walked. "Does anyone live here anymore?" she asked. "I can't see any roads or tracks or anything."

"I have not been here for years. When I was last here the abbey was occupied by about twenty monks. We shall see if they remain. There, look, the cottages."

The rough wattle and daub huts had fallen in on themselves, jagged walls remaining but the roofs long since vanished. It took no more than a few minutes for Cam to work his way through them. "Nothing," he said, rejoining her outside. "Let's try the abbey."

It took another hour to reach the abbey which was in little better condition than the cottages. The church roof had caved in, piles of stones lay covered in moss, the tiled floor slick with mold. The dormitory had fallen sideways, rotten wooden boards the only signs of the monks' beds.

"What happened here?" Rachel asked, picking up a stone and examining it before tossing it aside.

"The barefoot man," Cam replied. "I must see if anyone's here."

They searched together but there was no sign of life. The rain grew heavier, lashing down on the two of them as Cam's mood worsened. "The thief lied to us for a coin," he said at last. "There is no woman here."

"Then why did the barefoot man want to stop anyone coming to the island?"

"I dinnae ken but there is nothing else for us here."

"So we go back?"

Cam shook his head before pointing out to the waters of the loch. "See the froth. A storm grows and our boat is not strong. We would be dashed to pieces in minutes. We must ride out the storm. Come, the kitchen still has part of its roof. We will wait in there until the weather improves."

The weather did not improve. The wind grew into a gale, causing what was left of the roof above them to creak and groan. Drops of rainwater dripped continuously onto the floor.

Cam found a dry patch in the darkest corner and they huddled there together, waiting for so long that the sun faded from view.

"You should go home," he said, his voice loud to be heard over the gale blowing just a few feet away. "There's no one here." As he said it his arm went around her. "I shall miss you."

Rachel wasn't sure she heard him right over the wind and she dared not ask him to repeat it. She couldn't say anything. Did he like her? Was she wishing so strongly that she was putting words into his mouth that he wasn't saying. She listened in silence but he said nothing else.

"What will you do?" she asked, shifting closer to him, glad of the warmth of his body.

"Go back and defend the castle as best I can. God will have to decide whether I am worthy or not."

She felt for the necklace in her pocket. It called out to her to be used. Slowly, she let go of it again. "I'll go in the morning," she said, as much to herself as to Cam. "I couldn't leave you here all night. What kind of a guest would I be?"

"What kind of a host am I?" he asked. "I haven't exactly provided the best accommodation."

"It's all right. At least we're dry. Here, take some of this." She shuffled out of her coat, throwing it over the two of them.

"Your top," Cam said, looking at her arm. "It is torn."

"It's nothing. I'll fix it when I get back."

"What's that?" he asked, taking hold of her arm and pulling it gently toward him. "They look like burns."

"They are," she said quietly.

"Someone did this to you?"

She was going to lie like she usually did when people asked about the marks on her but the truth was out of her mouth before she knew what was happening. "Julia did it to me."

"Who's Julia?"

"My adoptive mom. The woman who raised me and my brother."

"She burned you?"

"With cigarettes. Little sticks that people set alight."

"And these?"

"The scars? Cuts with a kitchen knife."

"Your mother did these to you?"

She nodded. "Adoptive mother. I never knew my real mother. You know I've never admitted to anyone before what she did. Funny, now it's out, I'm not sure why I kept it in for so long."

"Why would she do that to you?"

"She wasn't a very nice person."

"I am sorry she hurt you."

"She's dead now. She can't hurt anyone anymore."

A silence fell between them for a minute. Cam held her tightly to his side, his hand stroking her arm softly.

"You have scars," Rachel said eventually. "More than me."

"These were from fights, not from my parents."

"You miss them, don't you?"

"The fights?"

"Your parents, silly."

"Aye. I miss them."

"How old were you when they died?"

"Ten."

She turned to look at him, his face little more than gray against black in the darkness. She could only see the slightest glint of his eyes, nothing more. "I'm sorry."

Before she knew what was happening his lips

were touching hers. He pulled away almost at once but the tingle remained as if they were still kissing. Her heart began to thump loudly in her chest as she leaned in for a second. He was no longer facing her, he was looking into the darkness.

"Did that just happen?" she asked, her hands trembling wildly as she ran them over her lips, her breath coming in rough gasps. "Did you just kiss me?"

"I shouldnae have done it. It willnae happen again."

"But why? Why did you kiss me? Where are you going."

He was on his feet. "To find us some food. You stay here. I will be back."

She sat alone in the darkness wondering if she'd done something wrong. It was the first kiss she'd ever experienced and it had come from nowhere. She was still experiencing it, her hands had yet to stop shaking. She felt more alive than ever.

Did it mean he liked her? It must. She felt his passion but then he sounded so angry afterward.

"People are confusing," she said out loud, wrapping the coat around herself once more.

When he came back he lit a fire, cooking a single scrawny pigeon. "It was all I could find in this storm," he said by way of explanation. "You have it."

"No, you should have it. I'll be going home in the morning."

"What if you stay?"

She looked up at him but his expression was as inscrutable as ever. "What do you mean?"

"What if you stay here?"

"With you?"

"Aye."

"And your clan that wants me dead?"

"I can talk them around."

"I don't know. Can I sleep on it?"

He grunted, turning his attention to the pigeon. Rachel shuffled close to the flames, warming her hands. The smoke ran along the roof and then vanished into the open. The wind continued to howl.

Cam steamed in the heat, the rainwater running down his chest. He said nothing else until the food was ready, passing her meat from the pigeon in chunks.

It was a small meal but it was better than nothing. She refused to eat it all, insisting that he take half. When they were done, they settled down together in the darkness.

Rachel lay on her side near the dying fire while Cam wrapped around her, his arm draped over her waist, pulling her tight to him.

"I want ye to stay," he whispered quietly in her ear.

She didn't answer. She didn't know what to say. She had spent so long not knowing how he felt and now he was telling her, she wasn't sure what to do. Could she stay in this time?

She lay with her eyes open in the dark and tried to weigh things up. Back home she had her academic career but little else. Sure, there were the modern comforts that she missed but then there were the other things she didn't miss.

All the noise, having to deal with her brother, not knowing if she'd ever earn enough to own her own house. If she stayed here what would she have? She'd still have no money. The clan wanted her dead.

Would he protect her like he said. Would he want to marry her? The thought made her heart race again. Imagine being with him for the rest of her life, feeling that sense of safety every time he touched her.

Her eyes began to close, feeling his breathing in

her ear. Whether he was awake or not she couldn't tell but she was soon asleep.

She dreamed she was back in Tallis, looking down on the boathouse. One of the boats was emerging onto the water. It had been patched up and the barefoot man was inside, rowing onto the stormy waters.

He didn't make it far before one of the huge waves washed over the side of the boat almost capsizing it. He kept going but more waves came and the boat began to slowly sink.

As she watched he was forced to swim back to the shore, looking out at the storm. She could tell what he was thinking. He was desperate to get to them both. She could only hope the storm lasted. She didn't want to think of what he might do if he caught up with them.

She stirred in her sleep, feeling Cam behind her. He planted a soft kiss on the back of her neck. With a contented sigh, she settled again, oblivious to the noise of the storm or to Cam's hands softly stroking the back of her hand as she slept on until dawn.

Chapter Fifteen

Cam was up before first light. He hadn't slept well. It wasn't because of the poor quality of the accommodation. He was used to sleeping in the open in the worst of conditions. He struggled to settle because he knew it was the last night he would get to spend with Rachel.

Something had happened to him since they'd met. He hadn't noticed it at first. It had crept up on him and by the time he realized what was going on, it was too late.

It was utterly ridiculous. It made no sense at all. Yet it kept him up for most of the night. It kept him breathing in her scent, listening to her slow and steady breathing when she finally settled from her bad dream. It made him ache in places he'd never known existed, deep inside his core. His soul had begun to yearn for her.

He was falling in love.

He barely knew her. He still didn't know if she was telling the truth about coming from the future. Who was he kidding? Of course she was telling the truth. She hadn't lied about a single thing since she'd arrived in his chamber those few short days ago. She had been honest with him about it all.

Was that why he felt a connection to her?

No one fell in love that fast. He was certain of that fact. Yet it had happened to him.

He lay in the dark wondering why he'd been so stupid as to kiss her. He might have been able to convince himself it was just a crush if he'd resisted kissing her.

But he couldn't resist. He had to do it. And it had been perfect. The world had stopped and everything faded away. There was just the two of them and everything had changed in that moment.

He could have kicked himself. It only made it harder that he was going to say goodbye to her in the morning. He should have kept his feelings to himself.

He had made a mistake, not one he would make

again. When he finally slept, he dreamed of nothing at all.

He woke up before her and was immediately on his feet. The storm had died down overnight. As the sun began to slowly rise, he looked out at the island. Water dripped through the ruins of the abbey, the sun sending sparkling whites and yellows across the water of the loch.

A thought occurred to him. He left Rachel asleep where she was, heading across the island to the jetty. He was right. The boat had been destroyed by the storm.

All that was left was a single hunk of wood still bound to the rope that he'd tied the night before. It bobbed in the water as if to mock him.

He looked across at the mainland. Could he swim across? It was a great distance, further than he had ever swum before. What choice did he have? It was that or live on the island in exile for the rest of his life.

He turned from the jetty, looking at the sandy beach to his left. There was something there that caught his eye. What was that?

The tide was going out leaving a strip of shale and sand that curved around to the left. That wasn't what drew his eye. It was the set of footprints that walked away out of sight. He made his way off the jetty to the beach, following the footsteps. Whoever made them had been barefoot. Had their nemesis made his way to the island overnight. Was Rachel in danger?

He picked up the pace, jogging after them toward a cave in the distance. The land rose around it, leaving a jagged gray stone cliff with a dark hole in the center. The footprints went into the hole and disappeared from sight.

With his sword drawn he headed inside. The waves echoed on the walls, making it hard to hear anyone or anything who might be hiding in there. Creeping forward he stopped, listening intently. Nothing.

Then a flicker of light in the distance. He approached slowly, sheathing his sword as he saw who was there. It was not the barefoot man. It was not a man at all. It was a woman with long white hair tied up neatly with twine.

She was sitting on a tree stump next to a roaring fire. The smoke rose and drifted away through a hole somewhere up above in the rocky ceiling of the cave.

"I've been waiting a long time to see you," the

woman said, turning to smile at him. "Come and join me. I have breakfast ready for you."

She passed him a fish from the fire as he walked slowly toward her. "Who are you?" he asked, taking the fish and biting into its side, spitting out the bones.

"You know who I am, don't you?"

"You're the one the thief talked about? You know how to defeat the barefoot man?"

"You can call me Morag. There will be time to answer all your questions soon but we must move. He is coming. We need to be ready to steal his boat for ourselves and get across to the mainland, leave him here to stew for a while."

"I willnae leave without Rachel."

"Who?" Morag looked shocked.

"The woman I came with."

"That makes things harder but not impossible." Morag talked more to herself than to him. "So be it. Bring her here and be quick about it. We do not have much time. I will cook for her while you're gone. Go, hurry."

Cam turned, heading out of the cave more confused than when he entered. How could the old woman have known he was coming?

As he emerged, he saw what she meant about

their enemy. In the distance his keen eyes spotted a rowing boat approaching, slowly drawing nearer. It would be some time before it arrived but he had to get back to the abbey and get Rachel to the cave before then. Would he be able to do it?

He broke into a run, not stopping until he was at the abbey. Rachel was not where he left her. There was no sign of her. He ran out of the kitchen into the open, scanning the grass. There, marks in the grass. She had gone that way. He darted after her, turning a corner before stopping dead.

She was standing with her back to him. She had removed her clothes and was washing herself with water from the well in the middle of the cloister. For the briefest of moments he was unable to move. She was stunningly beautiful, her back arched as she scrubbed at her arms.

Spinning on the spot, he looked the other way before calling her name, trying to force the image from his head. "Rachel."

There was a surprised squawk behind him before the rustling of clothing told him she was dressing as quickly as possible.

"How long were you watching me?" she asked, appearing beside him a minute later.

"No time for that," he said, grabbing her hand. "We need to move."

"Where are you taking me?" she asked as they ran.

"I found the woman we were looking for."

"What? Where?"

"A cave near the jetty. Come on, we need to get there before he does."

"Before who does? The barefoot man?"

"Aye. He's approaching the island as we speak."

By the time they got back to the cave, Rachel was out of breath. Cam watched her recover at the entrance to the cave while he glanced out at the water. The boat was getting too close for comfort. He could see the figure inside, his bald head reflecting the sunlight like a skull on a battlefield.

"Come on, inside," Cam said, pushing Rachel into the cave. She almost stumbled, regaining her feet in time to move into the darkness. With the shore hidden from view, Cam almost crashed into Morag who was standing with her hood over her head. She looked much like a monk in his cell, her hands the only things visible beside the fire.

"He is almost landed," Cam said. "Are you ready?"

She nodded. "Let him get ashore. He thinks you're at the abbey and he'll head straight there."

"Why should I not just run him through with my sword?"

"It would take much more than a sword to kill him. Dinnae worry though. I have a plan. Wait there. Rachel, there is a fish on the fire for you. Eat quick."

She moved toward the cave entrance, leaving Cam and Rachel alone. "Who is she?" Rachel asked.

"She said her name's Morag. I dinnae ken much about her but I get the feeling she has some powers that she has not yet used."

"Like what?"

"We shall have to wait to find out."

"Come on," Morag called back to them both. "Let's get moving."

They followed her outside to find her already untying the barefoot man's boat. There was a shout from further inland and they all looked in time to see the barefoot man running back toward them. "Get in," Morag snapped, holding out a hand to beckon Rachel aboard. "With haste."

Cam jumped in last, pushing the boat away from the jetty. The barefoot man was only a few feet away. Cam began to row as fast as he could, watching their attacker throw himself into the water, trying to swim out to them, hurling curses as he did so.

His head dipped under the water. He came up, took a gasping breath and then vanished again. He did not come back up.

"Is he dead?" Rachel asked. "Was it that simple? Is it over?"

"It will take a lot more than that to kill him but that buys us time."

Cam rowed silently across to the mainland. His mind kept shifting between two things. One was the vitriol in the barefoot man's face when he leapt into the water after them. It was a face that could not be reasoned with.

He could see for the first time why castles crumbled before that face. Even he balked at the idea of taking it on. It felt like he'd seen the face of a demon for the first time in his life.

He found himself glancing into the water, expecting to see him emerging, bursting into the boat to tear them all limb from limb.

His mind shifted from that to more pleasant memories. He thought of how Rachel had looked when he'd found her at the abbey, the softness of her skin, the way the light played in her hair, the way he wanted to run to her and sweep her into his arms.

He had panicked when he had been unable to find her because he feared she'd decided to go home after all without a chance of saying goodbye to her. He was glad she was still there, not wanting to ask her when she might go, fearing that would remind her she could leave at any time.

He desperately wanted her to stay even though he knew it was not possible for her to do so. She had her own life in her own time.

When they reached the mainland Cam was shocked to see the damage the storm had done to Tallis. Most of the houses had been destroyed, the villagers wandering aimlessly around, looking dazed, barely noticing them when they climbed out of their rowing boat.

"You picked the wrong side," Morag shouted to them. "See what happens to those who forsake the Lord for base fripperies."

"Have some compassion," Rachel replied, kneeling beside a crying child to comfort him. "Where's your mother?"

The boy pointed out at the water. "She was

swept away." He burst into fresh tears. "She's coming back, right?"

Rachel scowled up at Morag. "These are people," she snapped. "Just like you."

Morag muttered something under breath. "Very well," she said out loud, kneeling beside the boy. "Your mother will return to you." She put her hand on the boy's head and as she did so, someone shouted behind her.

Cam turned to see what the commotion was. A group of people were dragging someone from the water. For a moment he thought it was the barefoot man. Then he saw it was a spluttering and gasping woman who fell exhausted onto the shore.

"Mom!" the boy cried, getting to his feet and sprinting to the shore, throwing himself into her arms.

"Come," Morag said, tapping Cam on the shoulder. "We must be moving. We haven't much time."

"Where are we going?" Rachel asked, getting to her feet once more.

"If we're going to defeat him, there's only one way to do it."

"And what's that?"

"I need my spellbook."

Chapter Sixteen

The barefoot man had gone by many names in his time. As he sat in the ruins of the abbey, he decided the one he liked most was Michael. It was what the monks had called him when he first arrived on Kirrin Island. Abbot Michael. It had a nice ring to it.

If he wasn't so furious he might have smiled. Abbot Michael. That had been a pleasant couple of months, running the abbey into the ground, tempting as many of the monks into sin as he could possibly manage while lining his own pockets.

There was only one who failed him. Remigius. He had died when that wall mysteriously collapsed while he was supervising the repairs. Crushed to death under the stone on the day he finally realized who Abbot Michael really was. Such a shame but then, as the monks all said, it was clearly God's will that he was to die that day.

Things were simpler back then. They had become so much more complex since. He had come so close to her and yet things were not going the way he had planned. Something or someone had thrown a spanner in his works and he could guess who was interfering beyond his remit.

He looked up at the sky, a curse ready to emerge from his lips. That was when he saw the crow. It circled high in the sky, on the lookout for food. With a wave of his hand and a few muttered words, he brought the crow slowly toward him.

It circled lower and he waited patiently. He was a patient man. He had to be in his line of work.

Patience could only take him so far though. With all his neatly drawn out plans changing on an almost daily basis since she'd appeared, he was going to have to rethink.

It had been a simple enough scheme. Find the woman who came back in time, leapfrog on her to get into her era and then use his special set of skills to take over, finally get things done the way he wanted, use the technology he'd heard so much about, bring chaos to an entire world, not just a tiny little corner of it.

Everything had been planned in the correct manner. Yet somehow they were all still alive and he was trapped on the island. How had he not been able to foresee that?

He kept reliving the moment when he leaped into the water after them. So close to the rowing boat he could almost touch them. Then sinking down into the water as if something was pulling at him, dragging him under. He barely made it back to the shore with breath in his lungs.

He'd walked to the abbey, dripping all the way, knowing that the answer would come to him there as it had when he first heard about Morag's key. He just needed to stop the anger clouding his judgment.

The previous trip to the island had been under very different circumstances. He'd had the old woman brought here. It taught him a lesson. He wanted her to slowly starve to death, a pleasant torture for her trying to scupper his plans yet again.

Rachel was key to everything. He had tried to get hold of her when she was little and he'd been flummoxed that time by the key. He thought his chance was gone but his patience had worked in his favor. All these years later she was back and he had one more chance.

Then his shot had been snatched away because of Morag interfering once more. He wouldn't make any mistakes like that when he got his hands on her again. No slow starving to death on an island. No quips, no giving her the chance to escape. Straight in, get hold of her, murder her, then get hold of Rachel.

As for Cam? Well, he would either join the army of darkness or be trampled to death under it. The same went for his clan.

He managed a smile, thinking of how he might torture Morag and Cam in front of Rachel, then tell her the truth about everything, watch her little face crumble when she found out.

The crow came low enough for him to reach out an arm. It landed on the tip of his middle finger, looking at him blankly with eyes as cold as his own. A single caw then it was silent, waiting.

Leaning forward, he whispered into the crow's ear for a moment before sending it flying upward once again. The message would reach the villagers soon enough and then they'd row out to get him.

They knew what would happen if he was left there much longer. He wouldn't leave any of them alive. The protection he'd given them was already on the precipice. They had one job. How hard was that? Lock up the woman and anyone with her. Simple enough yet they hadn't even managed to do that properly.

He sat and waited, feeling his hunger grow. A rabbit limped slowly closer across the grass. It was clearly injured and struggling to walk. He watched it impassively, his mind on other things.

Kill Morag. Kill Cam. Get the necklace from Rachel. Get to her time and take over. Simple enough. Maybe make her his bride for a while. She was pretty enough to look at and she looked like she'd be easily cowed. He'd probably only have to threaten her a bit before she did what he said. He might hit her just for fun but he wouldn't need to be too violent. She was cowed already.

He knew the type. Rough childhood. It made for a nice easy to manipulate adult. Maybe he could get her to bring a son into the world. Was the world ready for that? Father and son in charge. The thought made him laugh out loud.

The rabbit looked up at the sound. He leaned down, tearing a hunk of grass and waving it gently toward the rabbit. "Come on, come and get it. I won't hurt you, little one."

The rabbit hopped closer, unsure, sniffing the air, limping as it moved.

"Come on," he said again. "That's it."

The rabbit took another couple of uneasy steps, sniffing at the grass in his hand. With a scoop of his hand, he lifted the tiny bunny upward before breaking its neck and swallowing it whole.

He laughed again.

Capturing her would be just as easy. He might have had hurdles put in his way but that only made the challenge that bit more interesting. He licked his lips. He could almost taste her. Soon enough she would be in his grasp and all would be right with the world.

He'd swept the Highlands in search of her and he'd finally found her. Taking the castles and destroying the clans had been fun but now he had a new goal. Burning the land, salting the earth, that was just a warm up for the real task. Getting her.

He was so close to the future, he could almost picture it. What would the world be like when he got there?

He had seen many changes in his time. Lost for so long after his last failure but now so close to success he could taste it. He would make the MacGregors pay for what their ancestors did to him. He would swallow their future like he had the rabbit.

Whatever it was like, it would soon bend to his will just like the snack he'd just enjoyed. Bend to his will or be destroyed.

Who said he never gave anyone a choice?

Chapter Seventeen

R achel walked a few feet behind the
other two as they talked. Cam had a lot
of questions about the barefoot man
and Morag, as she called herself, had answers for all
of them.

Rachel was happy to be ignored for the time
being. It gave her time to think. She fingered the
necklace in her pocket, thinking again how easily
she could go home if she wanted to. She could be
away from all this danger, get warm and dry.

They walked for an hour through a fine
morning before the wind began to grow. Passing
through a gully between two mountains, it whistled
through them, sending a chill deep into her.

She wrapped her coat around her, watching as

Cam continued to walk as if the wind wasn't even there. He was a machine more than a person, designed for these kind of conditions. Unlike her.

She glanced across at Morag just in time to see her hood slip back, revealing her face. She only caught a glimpse but she could have sworn she knew that face from somewhere. But where? Had it maybe been in one of her history books? Had she seen a portrait somewhere?

They passed out of the gully and into the open. A burned village lay to their left, the fire long turned to ashes, the remains of the houses little more than stumps. Even the strips of crops had been burned. Nothing remained at all.

"Did he do that?" Morag asked Cam.

"Aye," he replied. "He has torched much of the land between here and MacGregor territory. We must be cautious. His spies are everywhere."

"Things have changed much since he arrived and none of it for the better."

"Where did he come from?" Rachel asked, catching up with the two of them. "I haven't read about him in any of my books."

"You know how to read?"

"Of course I do."

"I see. And what books have you read about this?"

"Plenty. I've read all about the history of Scotland."

"What good is learning history when the things we discuss are happening right now?"

Cam took over. "She is not from this time."

"What?" Morag looked shocked, examining the two of them closely. "I warn you, now is not the time for jests."

"No jests. She appeared in my tower out of thin air from several hundred years hence."

"Extraordinary. The prophecy continues to run its tendrils through the world, I see. So, future woman. What do you know about this time?"

"I know that there's no mention of any barefoot man sweeping the Highlands, taking over the clans, burning the land."

"That bodes well. That means we still have time."

"What?" Cam asked. "What are you talking about?"

She didn't get a chance to answer. From the gully behind them came the thundering of hooves. Rachel turned in time to see half a dozen people riding toward them, swords held high. "His people?" Cam asked.

"No," Morag replied. "He would not send so few. They come hunting for something different. Hurry, come this way."

"We cannot outrun them," Cam replied, drawing his sword. "Take Rachel and get out of here."

"Come with us," Rachel replied, tugging at his arm.

"We would be cut down together if I did. Take care of yourself." He swept her into his arms, planting a passionate kiss on her lips. She barely knew it was happening before it was over. "Now go!"

He turned to face the horses, his sword held high. Morag grabbed Rachel's hand and dragged her away but she fought herself free.

She looked back in time to see the horses surrounding Cam. She felt certain he would be killed but there were too many of them crowding him and none had room to deal a fatal blow.

She could do nothing but watch things unfold. He swung his sword from left to right, fending the attackers off. "We will sacrifice her," one yelled. "And you shall not stop us."

Two rode away from the group, heading toward Rachel. She screamed as their horses thundered across the trail. Morag stepped in front of her, muttering something under her breath.

At once the horses stopped dead, throwing their riders. The two men thumped to the ground as their steeds turned tail and galloped away.

"Stay behind me," Morag said, drawing a sword out from under her cloak. She pointed it toward the two dazed men. "Go while you can," she said.

They took one look at each other and then laughed. "Come on then, Granny," one said. "Let's see what you've got."

They lunged at the same time but she was far faster than they guessed. Neatly moving forward instead of back, she got past them, spinning on her heels and jabbing one with the tip of her blade, catching his ankle and nicking it deep enough for blood to spurt onto the grass under him.

He fell at once, screaming and clutching at the wound as his colleague looked less certain than moments earlier.

Rachel's gaze moved to Cam who was gaining the upper hand over the remaining four. One man was slumped on the ground and Cam was on his horse, drawing the remaining three away.

Morag motioned for her attacker to come toward her and he roared, diving forward with his sword but overreaching, falling to his knees as he lost his balance.

Before he could right himself, her sword was in the back of his neck. His roar turned into a gurgle as he twisted sideways, falling next to his companion, never to move again.

Morag ran over to Rachel, not seeing the wounded man shifting on the ground. "Look out!" Rachel shouted but it was too late.

The man raised a dagger at the same time as Morag turned. Her sword plunged into him at the same time as he threw the dagger, his blade striking Morag in the chest. It wedged there as he slumped down dead. She fell, looking down in shock at the hilt sticking out of her.

"No!" Rachel shouted, kneeling beside her, holding her in her arms.

"What happened?" Cam asked, riding over. She looked past him. The other horses were galloping away, their riders no longer fancying their odds against such a skilled sword master.

"She's dying," Rachel said. "There's too much blood."

"Is there nothing we can do?"

Morag opened her mouth to speak but nothing came out.

"She might have a chance," Rachel said, pulling out the necklace. "Here, take this and wrap your hands around it." She slid the necklace over Morag's head. "When you get there, call for help."

Morag reached up, stroking Rachel's cheek. "You must get the spellbook," she whispered, coughing up blood as she did so. "Save the past to save your future."

"Where is it?" Cam asked, climbing down from his horse. "Where is the spellbook?"

"My house is due east of here. Follow the trail and you'll find it. Go to the marked page and learn the spell. Take the book with you to the stone circle at Cullen Point. You must get there before the full moon if you're to stand a chance." She coughed up more blood, wincing as she did so.

"Go," Rachel said, moving Morag's hands toward the necklace. "Before it's too late."

Morag grabbed hold of the necklace, pressing it to her chest. An instant later she was gone, like she had never been there.

"What just happened?" Cam asked. "Where did she go?"

"To my time," Rachel replied. "I only hope we weren't too late."

"Come on," Cam said, helping her to her feet. "They will be back soon, and in greater numbers. We must ride swiftly. The full moon is due this night."

"You think what she said will work?"

"I've just seen a woman disappear into thin air. I dinnae ken what is real and what isnae anymore."

He lifted her up onto the horse before climbing behind her. She could feel his chest against her back, his arms holding her tight as he took the reins and led them away from the corpses of their attackers.

"How will you get back without the necklace?" he asked as they began to ride.

"We'll worry about that later. For now let's concentrate on getting the spellbook."

They stuck to the trail for sometime until Cam heard a noise behind them. Looking back he could see nothing. Nonetheless, he quickly turned the horse into the grass toward a copse of trees in the distance.

When they reached them, he stopped, climbing straight off the horse into a tree and looking back the way they came.

"They are hunting us," he said.

"Hunting me, you mean. I heard them talking about sacrificing me."

"You should have gone home while you had the chance."

"Then she'd be dead and you'd be alone."

"At least you wouldn't be risking your life."

"You risked yours to save me. And that kiss by the way. Are we going to talk about that or do you want to pretend it never happened again?"

"I thought I might never see you again. I couldnae let you go without a goodbye kiss. It wouldnae be polite, would it?"

"So you did that out of politeness?"

"Not quite. Look, over there. I see her house."

"How do you know it's hers?"

"Hidden in the trees. She meant us to find it this way. I see the thatch, it blends well with the leaves. She was clearly good at hiding things."

He climbed back down, leading the horse slowly through the trees until they saw a clearing in the centre of the copse. Cam stopped the horse by a gnarled ash tree.

"I dinnae like it," he said. "There's something making my skin crawl."

A moment later the door of the cottage opened

and two men stepped out, both holding wicked looking axes.

"Wait here," Cam said, motioning for Rachel to stay hidden. He tied the horse to the nearest tree before climbing down.

She watched as he moved to the left, scanning the ground as he went. He leaned down, picked up a stone, and then hurled it toward the far side of the cottage. It landed with a thud and the two men looked that way, heading toward the trees on the far side of the clearing.

Cam crossed the space to the cottage like the quietest wind, darting inside and out of sight. Rachel held her breath, waiting for him to emerge.

The guards finished their sweep and returned, seeing the open door and walking inside, axes ready in front of them. She barely had time to react before Cam emerged. Blood was dripping down his face as he walked slowly over, a heavy leather bound book in his hand, his sword sheathed. He was not even out of breath.

How could she have fallen for him? He looked like what he was, a murderous brute from a violent time. She couldn't possibly stay in a time when people were being slaughtered on what seemed like a daily basis.

"Come on," he said, wiping the blood from his face with the back of his hand. "Let's get to the stone circle."

"You know where it is?" she asked, trying to ignore her revulsion.

"Aye. Cullin Point is not far from here." He glanced up at the sky. "We should make it before nightfall."

The horse made the journey a lot quicker. Once Rachel got used to riding it, she almost enjoyed it. Her pleasure was lessened knowing she was stuck in the Middle Ages with a killer. There would be no way back.

"Maybe there's a spell in here that can get you home," Cam said, tapping the book she was gripping tightly between her hands. "I didnae get chance to read it."

"How do you know it's the right book?"

"It was the only one in there."

"What did you do, to those men I mean?"

"Dealt with them."

He refused to be drawn into the matter so Rachel dropped it, concentrating on not letting go of the book. "What do I do if there isn't a spell that'll get me home?"

"Philip will ken a way tae dae it."

"How do you know?"

"He knows much more than me about such things. Look, there's the circle."

In a long open stretch of heather, a jagged circle of rough gray stones pointed up at the sky. They rode toward it, dismounting the horse at the edge and leaving it enjoying the few tufts of grass that lay between the masses of heather. "Find the spell," Cam said, turning to look at Rachel.

"Yes," a voice said from the far side of the circle. "Find the spell, Rachel."

They both looked as from behind the tallest stone the barefoot man emerged. "How did you get here so fast?" Cam asked, walking slowly toward him.

"That's not the question you should be asking. The question you should be asking is what happens if you take another step toward me?"

From behind other stones more men appeared, all of them grinning wickedly at Cam. He paused, calculating his odds.

"I wouldn't," the barefoot man said. "Their bows move faster than your sword." He turned his attention to Rachel as Cam stood glaring at him. "If you give me the book, I'll tell you the spell that will send you home."

"If you know it, why haven't you used it?" she asked, gripping the book tighter.

"Oh, aren't you a clever one?" He took a step toward her. Cam blocked his path. He stopped, looking indifferent. "The spell needs you just as the necklace needs you. You're the key to all of this, don't you understand?"

"I understand you need to leave us alone before I cast the spell that deals with you once and for all."

"You could do that. Or you could give me the book and I'll tell you who your birth mother is. How does that sound for a deal? The answer to the question you've always wanted to know. Who are your parents? Give me the book and I'll tell you."

"Dinnae do it," Cam said, turning to plead with her. "He's lying."

She took a step forward, loosening her grip on the book. "That's it," the barefoot man said, reaching out, beckoning her on. "Bring it here. You're doing the right thing."

She stopped, opening the book and looking down at one blank page after another, flicking through them all. "There are no spells in here."

"Bring it here," he said, snapping at her. "The moon will soon rise and the writing will be visible."

"Look," she said, seeing the page marked with a bookmark. *Bensons - Best for Books.* "What's this?"

"Never mind that," the barefoot man said. "Give me the book of your own free will and together we can rule the world."

Rachel's eyes scanned down the page. The words formed together, ink running into lines across the page. The words meant nothing but she read them out anyway, the words echoing loudly around the clearing.

"No," the barefoot man said, running toward her. "Stop. You don't know what you're doing."

Cam leapt on him and then everything happened at once. The other men pulled their bows, arrows flying toward Cam. The barefoot man couldn't get past him, scrambling to free himself from Cam's grip.

She said the last words of the spell and there was a flash of light so bright it burned her eyes. It came from the book, filling the clearing. The light died almost as soon as it came. The barefoot man was gone.

The arrows were broken and bent on the floor, the men turning and running, praying loudly for their souls, fleeing the sight of such witchcraft. Cam was no longer holding the barefoot man. Instead,

THE KEY IN THE LOCH

his arms were wrapped around a tall stone that hadn't been there a moment ago.

"I thought you were going to give him the book," Cam said, letting go of the stone before tapping it with his finger. "Is that him?"

"I think so," she replied, closing the book.

"How did you know that spell would work?"

"I didn't but all the other pages were blank."

"So no spell to get you home then?"

"I think he might have been able to read it even though we can't."

Cam frowned. "What makes you say that?"

"I just get a feeling about it. Now, you said Philip might know another way to get me home."

"Aye."

"Then we better go see him, hadn't we."

Cam picked up one of the fallen arrows. "I thought I was dead for sure." He tossed it back to the ground. "Come on then. If our horse hasn't wandered off on his own, we should be back home by tomorrow night."

Chapter Eighteen

They spent that night together sleeping under the stars. The weather was warmer than it had been since she arrived.

"The chill grip on the land is fading," Cam said, feeling the soil under his fingertips. "He no longer has a hold on the Highlands."

"Is he really gone, do you think?" Rachel asked.

"He's been turned into solid stone. I doubt he'll cause us any more trouble."

"What about his followers?"

"Whatever spell they were under has broken. You saw the speed they ran from the stone circle."

"So it's really over?"

Cam nodded, rolling onto his side and tapping

the ground next to him. "Aye, I think it is. And all thanks to you."

Rachel nestled into the space in front of him, feeling as safe as always with his arms wrapped around her. She was going to miss him. He might be a brute and a killer but she was still going to miss him.

She did not remember her dreams the next morning, if she had them at all. She woke up feeling refreshed. Cam was right about the atmosphere. It felt better. The air was crisper, the light brighter. The darkness that had spread was dissipating with the morning mist, hopefully never to return.

That day they saw many signs of life. New flowers were blooming through the soil where there had been only scorched earth before. Crops were beginning to sprout.

The sun beating down upon the two of them, forcing them to rest often. They drank from streams as did their horse, the water ice cold and a blessed relief from the heat of the sun.

In the afternoon Cam bathed in a loch, swimming out into the water while Rachel washed at the edge of the shore. When he emerged a short time later, his hose clung to him in such a way that she had to look away, blushing as she did so.

She needed to focus. Thinking about that outline of his body through his hose wouldn't help. She couldn't stay. She knew that. She didn't belong in this time. She belonged at home in her own time.

If she stayed she would only cause problems for him. Already she had caused conflict between the MacKenzies and the MacGregors.

He came and sat beside her on the shore, water dripping from his hair. "You ready to move on?" he asked. "We will be there in a couple of hours."

"I'm ready," she said, feeling far from it. The day was slipping by too fast. When they got there, she would find a way home and have no excuse not to use it. Then she would be alone again.

Sure, she would have her memories of Cam and of the Highlands but that would be a pale imitation of true happiness. And she had found happiness with him, for those brief moments when he kissed her, when he held her close at night, she was happier than she'd ever been before.

She thought of the battles they'd come through, the blood spilled, the people killed. Could she stay knowing that more deaths might occur, deaths for which she might be responsible? Was she bad luck? Was that what it was?

She remained lost in thought until they reached the castle. By the time it came into view she'd made up her mind. She didn't want to go. She would wait for the right moment to talk to him about it but the right moment wasn't when the trumpets were ringing and the portcullis was being raised, the occupants of the castle coming out to greet the safe return of their Laird.

"Philip," Cam said, spotting him through the crowd. Rachel looked but saw nothing. She looked again and there he was, almost hidden against the stone walls. He walked through the crowd, taking Cam's outstretched hand. "It is good to see you alive."

"I could say the same about you. How goes it?"

"I bring my betrothed back alive." He kissed Rachel before turning back to the crowd. "And the barefoot man is now a stone man."

"A stone man?"

"Part of the stone circle at Cullen Point."

"But how?"

"A spell-"

Another voice interrupted. "I told you. She is a witch. She must be sacrificed."

Rachel looked to see the owner of the voice. It was Tor, he was pointing at her, his face red as he yelled once more. "She brought us this evil. We must burn her."

"She saved us all," Cam said, having to raise his voice to make it heard over the crowd. "It is because of her that the barefoot man is gone forever."

"Lies!"

The crowd grew closer, hands reaching out for Rachel. Cam pushed as many away as he could but he could not hold back the tide for long. "Take her somewhere safe," he yelled to Philip, drawing his sword and using the butt of it to keep people at bay.

Rachel felt hands clawing at her. She pushed back as people spat the word, "Witch," into her face.

"Come on," Philip said, grabbing her arm and yanking her through the crowd. "Say nothing."

As soon as they were in the mass he threw a cloak over her, moving her slowly away from the crowd until they were at the base of the wall. "What are you doing?" Rachel hissed from under the hood.

"Getting you somewhere safe, like he said."

Philip moved silently, leading her toward the

corner and then onto a thin rabbit trail that moved up the hillside into the woods beyond. She looked back, seeing the crowd still surrounding Cam.

"We must help him," she said, trying to turn Philip around.

"He can look after himself well enough. All he needs is to deal with Tor. The man is a serpent."

"Why do they think I'm a witch?"

"He's been whispering in their ears the entire time you've been gone, talking about you bewitching Cam. Then when he kissed you that was all the proof they needed. They listened too much to his whispered words. Cam will set them straight soon enough if he deals with Tor first. Until then we need to get you back to your own time. To be sure you will be safe"

"What? How do you know about that?"

"That you're from the future? I have ears in many places. I know the necklace brought you here. I also know where there is another one."

"Where?"

"This way."

He led her through the woods and out the other side. The castle vanished from sight in the distance behind them. Eventually, they reached an abandoned village, houses covered with ivy, others half rotten and falling into the earth.

"What happened here?" Rachel asked. "Was it the barefoot man?"

"No. It was abandoned after the last war, too hard to defend. The people fled to the castle after the fire. This is the place." He stopped in the doorway of one of the more complete buildings. It still had three walls and half of its thatch roof, the straw green and stinking, the smell sticking to Rachel's throat as they entered.

Philip knelt down in the corner, levering up a small flagstone. Using it as a spade, he began to scrape away at the earth, not stopping until he uncovered a small wooden box. He brushed the soil from it as he lifted it into the open.

"Let me see that," Rachel said, taking it from him. "This is the box that came to my house. How's that possible?"

"I don't know," he replied.

"Where did it come from? How did you know it was down there?"

"It was hidden during the war to stop them from stealing the necklace. Someone told me it would be needed one day."

"Who?" She pulled at the lid. "It's locked."

"The key is back at the castle. I wish I'd known this would happen. I'd have brought it with me. Come on, we will have to try and retrieve the key without anyone noticing."

They made their way back toward the castle. Rachel carried the box, her head spinning. At some point the box was buried and then dug up in the distant past. Then it made its way to her. Someone posted it to her but who? More importantly, why?

She couldn't make head nor tail of the matter. She could only hope to find the answers at some point in the future.

When they got back to the castle the crowd had gone as had Cam. "Inside somewhere," Philip said. "No doubt sorting all this out. We will go through the sally port and into the tower. The key is in the muniments room behind a loose stone. Come, quickly, before the guards spot you. We do not yet know where their loyalties lie."

They moved to the base of the wall, hugging the stone so they could not be viewed from the battlements. Philip led her around to the sally port. "This is how we left last time," she said, thinking how much had changed since then.

"Keep quiet," he replied, pulling out a key and unlocking the door. They slipped through it and into the tunnel beyond. At the end they stopped, Philip peering out. "Wait," he said. "There are too many people."

She looked past him, seeing Cam at the far side of the courtyard. At least he didn't look hurt. The crowd had vanished. He must have gained control while they were gone. Or had he told them the witch had been dealt with and they were safe once more?

She looked at him more closely. He was in the middle of a conversation with a beautiful woman almost as tall as him. She'd never seen her before but she couldn't stop feeling a pang of jealousy as the woman put her hand on Cam's arm.

To her surprise the woman leaned up and kissed Cam. Everyone in the courtyard turned to watch.

Rachel's insides churned as she saw what was happening. "Come on," Philip said. "While they're distracted."

She followed him out into the open. They moved quickly up the keep steps and inside. Philip walked up another flight of stairs and then along a narrow corridor. Rachel followed, unable to get what she'd seen out of her head. He kissed someone else. Was that the woman he was supposed to marry?

She couldn't remember her name but she remembered the MacKenzies talking about the woman he'd turned down, the friction that had caused.

"How did you calm them all down?" Rachel asked as Philip unlocked another door. "When we went, I mean?"

"It wasn't difficult. The MacKenzies are like children. You just need to know how to handle them. As for the MacGregors, well they can be children themselves sometimes. If it wasn't for Tor they would have been as quiet as lambs. Instead, he turned them into wild boars."

He pushed the door open and headed inside. Rachel followed him in time to see him pull the loose stone from the wall. There was the key she knew so well with its intricate M carved into the handle.

She took the key from him and unlocked the box, pulling out the necklace. It was deep blue like the clear waters of a loch. The blue seemed to swirl and shift in the light like waves falling on a misty shore. "It's time to go home," she said, thinking of Cam kissing the woman outside.

"Are you ready?" Philip asked, taking the open box from her.

"One last look outside," she said, crossing to the narrow window in the far wall. "I'm going to miss this place." She took a final glance at everything she was going to leave behind. She wouldn't just miss the castle. She'd miss the mountains, the smell of the air, the wonderful clothes they all wore.

What was that?

She looked down at the courtyard. There was a huge pile of wood being stacked ever higher.

"What's happening down there?"

Philip leaned past her, shouting down. "What's the fire for?"

"We are going to sacrifice the Laird."

Rachel's blood ran cold. She staggered back from the window. Philip turned to look at her. "This isn't your fight," he said. "You can go home right now and forget about all of this."

Rachel looked at the necklace and then up at Philip. Go home and leave Cam to be burned by his own people? Or stay and what? Try and save him and probably burn too?

She took a deep breath and then ran out of the muniments room, getting down to the courtyard in under a minute.

"Stop," she yelled as a struggling Cam was

dragged toward the pile of wood. "He saved you all and this is how you repay him?"

They all turned to look at her. "The barefoot man is coming," Tor shouted. "He demands a sacrifice and we must provide it."

"The barefoot man is gone," she replied.

"Prove it," someone shouted.

"The proof is in the air. Can you not taste how sweet it is? Look out there and see the crops and flowers grow once again."

"Sacrifice him!" Tor screamed. "Now!"

"If you must sacrifice anyone, make it me."

"Very well," Tor replied. "You can burn together. Take hold of her."

Strong arms grabbed her and dragged her over to the fire. She fought them but they were too strong, lifting and tying her beside Cam. A silence fell over the courtyard.

Then Rachel's cellphone rang.

The crowd looked left and right, trying to identify the strange sound emanating from her pocket.

"What is that?" Tor asked, eyeing her suspiciously, a flaming torch in his hand ready to set the wood ablaze.

"Someone must have hit the on button," she replied. "Untie me and I can answer it."

Tor shook his head but someone was already climbing the wood, undoing the bonds that held her hands in place. She reached at once into her pocket and brought out the cellphone, hitting the green button on the screen. The battery flashed a warning sign as she did so. "Hello?"

"Put me on speaker," said the voice of Morag from the other end of the line. "With haste."

Rachel did as she was asked and Morag's voice boomed out, louder than Rachel would have thought possible. "The prophecy spoke of many things," she said. "It spoke of a voice from a box, a voice that must be obeyed."

A murmur spread through the crowd. More than a couple of people crossed themselves.

"Release the Laird. Release the woman. Beg their forgiveness."

The crowd threw themselves on the floor. All of them supplicating themselves except Tor who continued to brandish the torch.

"What is that?" he asked, looking closer at the cellphone. "Some new witchcraft?"

The others by Tor's side grabbed him, pulling him to the floor. The torch rolled away, the flames dying in the thick mud of the courtyard.

"Forgive us," one voice cried, soon joined by many others. "Forgive us all."

"Take me off speaker," the voice said. Rachel put the phone to her ear as two men ran up the pile of wood, untying the remaining ropes that held the two of them in place.

"Morag?" She asked. "Is that you?"

"Aye. It's me. Though you can call me ma."

Rachel almost fell over at hearing those words. "What?" The low battery warning beeped in her ear.

"I'm your mother, Rachel."

"But-"

"We haven't much time. The key must be thrown into the loch. I will see you-" The cellphone went dead.

"Mom, I love you," It was too late. She was gone.

"That was your mother?" Cam asked, rubbing his wrists where the ropes had cut into his flesh. "How is that possible?"

"I don't know," she replied. "But can we get off this bonfire before we talk about it?"

The still grovelling people moved aside to let them pass. The entire atmosphere of the castle had changed.

"Where's Tor?" Cam asked, looking around him. "Where is that swine?"

No one had seen him. Cam organized a search party before taking Rachel into the keep and then up to his chamber. He sat in the chair in the corner while she perched on the edge of the bed, holding the necklace in her hand.

"So you could have gone home at any time yet you joined me on the bonfire?" he asked. "Why?"

"I couldn't let them burn you," she replied. "Look, I know you love someone else but I had to save you before I went."

"What? Love someone else? Who?"

"Oh, don't bother pretending. I saw you kissing her in the courtyard."

"Alice? She was trying to get me to agree to marry her but I'm not in love with her."

"But the kiss?"

"I pushed her away, Rachel. There's only one person I love and it is not Tor's sister. She said if I married her, she'd get him to stop them all, persuade them no sacrifice was needed."

"And you refused?"

"I would rather burn than marry one I do not love."

"So you don't love her?"

He smiled, getting to his feet and crossing the room, taking her hands in his. "There is only one woman I love and have always loved."

"And who's that?"

"The woman sitting in front of me." He lifted her to her feet. "I love you, Rachel. Could you ever love me?"

"You just try and stop me," she replied, jumping into his arms.

He kissed her then and he did not stop. His lips pressed against hers as they held each other in the bedchamber.

"I thought I'd lost you," he said between embraces. "That you would go back to your own time and I would never see you again."

"No such luck," she replied. "You're stuck with me now whether you like it or not."

"Och, I like it," he said, his smile broadening as he moved her across to the bed. "I like it very much indeed."

Chapter Nineteen

"Will they find him?" Cam asked.

Philip raised an eyebrow in response. "Of course they will. He can't hide forever."

Cam leaned back in his seat, taking a deep breath before speaking again. "Thank you, that will be all."

Philip nodded before turning, leaving Cam alone in the great hall.

Tor and Alice had vanished together. In the weeks since their disappearance Cam had been able to piece together exactly why the clan had been so hard to manage.

Tor, his trusted Man-at-Arms, the clan member responsible for vetting newcomers and protecting the castle. In league with the barefoot man. It shocked him to find out the truth. Tor and his sister had worked together for months to undermine Cam's control, planting rumors, whispering in ears, maintaining contact with the villain.

Worst of all was finding out that Tor had killed Mistress Abernathy. One of the servant's found Tor's ring between two of the barrels in the stores, a drop of dried blood still stuck to the stone.

Philip had taken over Tor's role, sending out several patrols to hunt for him while also looking after the castle. The only problem was the patrols were manned with men trained by Tor. He knew better than them where they would look.

Would he evade justice for good? Philip seemed certain he would be caught but Cam was not so sure.

"Hey," a voice said, interrupting his thoughts.

He looked up and managed a smile as Rachel walked across the room toward him. "Good morning," he said, holding out a hand to her.

She sat beside him, planting a kiss on his cheek. "I'm not sure I'll ever get used to you getting up so early and leaving me alone in bed."

"I have much to do to heal my people. They are drowning in shame for the way they treated us."

"And you could have punished them severely but you did not."

"My father always said you win more people over with sweetmeats than with branding irons."

"We have something similar. You win over more people with honey over vinegar. I'm glad you're that person, not the vengeance type."

"Did you think I was some mindless brute?"

"For a while, yes. But there's more to you than that. I saw you giving those sword lessons to Roger."

"The spitboy? Well, there's nae harm in having more trained men guarding the castle."

She smiled, poking him in the side. "I knew it. There's a nurturing father figure in there after all."

"Dinnae tell anyone." He smiled.

"Your secret's safe with me. Are you ready to get going?"

"Aye, and it's a grand day for traveling."

Cam stood up and took Rachel in his arms, holding her tight and breathing in the scent of her hair. She always smelled so good.

Together, they made their way out into the courtyard where the horses were waiting.

Rachel had been learning to ride but for a journey of this length she still preferred to sit with

Cam on his horse. He didn't mind. It gave him the chance to hold her close and think about all the things he wanted to do to her.

The journey to Tallis was much quicker by horse than on foot. They were there by the end of the day. The sun was setting when they reached the village, the water of the loch beyond it still. It was a warm evening. Most of the villagers were done for the day, sitting together on the grass and talking excitedly about the upcoming consecration.

Morag's words had cut deep with them all when she landed from exile. They had come to a decision since she went. The abbey was to be rebuilt, the villagers providing the labor. Work had begun and at midnight the bishop, who'd come all the way from Stirling, would reconsecrate the church and give his blessing to the endeavor.

With the arrival of Cam, things swung into action. The line of rowboats along the shore began to fill with people. Cam took the last of the boats with Rachel, the two of them following the twinkling lights that spread out across the water in front of them.

"How does it feel tae be back here?" he asked as he pushed the oars deep into the water.

"Strange," Rachel replied. "I miss her, you know?"

"Aye. I ken you do. I get the feeling you will see her again someday though."

"You do?"

"Aye."

"I was so close to my mother and I didn't even know it was her until it was too late." She was silent for a moment. "At least she survived that knife wound."

"I would have sworn such a thing was fatal."

"Medicine's come a long way."

"You still happy you stayed? Don't want tae go back tae your own time?"

She reached across and put her hand on his. He stilled the oars for a moment, letting the boat rock gently on the water. "I made my decision," she said. "And it was the right one. Is this just your way of saying you want to get rid of me?"

He laughed. "I dinnae think I could get rid of you if I tried. And I did try."

"Yes you did."

He resumed rowing, reaching the island not long after the others. They could tell where they were by the lights heading into the distance. Cam didn't follow them, instead taking Rachel's hand

and leading her across the beach to the cave. Inside everything was as he had arranged.

"What's this?" Rachel asked, looking at the blanket lit by candles, the food arranged neatly in baskets. "Did you do this?"

"Aye. I thought we could be alone together for a while. It's hard enough getting away from my people tae spend time with you."

"What about the consecration? The bishop will be waiting."

"He can wait a little longer. First I want you to sit down so I can ask you something."

Rachel sat cross legged on the blanket as Cam reached into his pocket and brought out a ring. He got down on one knee and held the ring out toward her.

"What's this?" she asked. "What are you doing?"

"I ken when you first came I pretended you were my betrothed. I ken that we told our people after that it wasnae the truth. Now I want that tae be the truth, a truth that is as solid as my love for you, as solid as these stone walls that surround us.

"I love you, Rachel Fisher. I want you as my bride. If you agree tae our union, I swear I will spend the rest of my life showing you just how strong my love for you is. Will you marry me?"

She looked down at the ring and then up at him. For a moment he thought she might say no. There was no smile on her face.

"I can't believe it," she said at last. "You really want to marry me?"

"Of course I do. Did you no think I did?"

"No, it's just, I didn't think anyone would ever want to marry me."

"And no one will if you no say yes."

"Will your people approve?"

"They love you as much as I. They've seen the land coming back to life, the darkness fading away. The prophecy said the one with the box must be obeyed. They will never question you, nor hurt you. Neither will I if you would make me the happiest Highlander in all of Scotland. Say you will."

She beamed, throwing herself on him and flattening him on the ground. "Yes, of course, yes!"

He kissed her then, a kiss that bonded the two of them together far stronger than any ring ever could.

When they eventually emerged from the cave, Rachel wore the ring on her finger.

They made it to the abbey just in time. A new track had been beaten into the earth and it was impossible to get lost. The villagers were aligned before the altar. The rubble had been cleared away, piled up in the open. The first courses of the new church had been built, enough to show the outline of the building.

It was going to be glorious, Cam could tell just by examining the work so far. The stones were aligned with great skill.

At the altar, the bishop stood waiting. When he saw Cam he began to speak. "We are gathered here today to consecrate sacred ground to the Lord, our God. With this ceremony darkness and sin is expunged from the very earth around us.

"This space will remain sacred for as long as there are people to till the earth and pray to the Lord, seeking nothing for themselves but forgiveness for their own sins and those of their fellow countrymen."

Cam felt Rachel's hand slide into his. The two of them looked across the crowd, the yellow glow of many torches illuminating the interior of the church. A light breeze blew but it was fresh rather than oppressive.

Cam felt as if all the pain and hardship of the

last few months had been worth it for this one perfect moment.

She had said yes.

The bishop continued his speech and Cam did his best to listen but his mind could only focus on the fact that the stunningly beautiful woman beside him was going to be his wife.

She had the chance to go back to the time where she belonged and instead she had chosen to stay with him.

The necklace was locked away in the box. She said she dared not risk wearing it in case it sent her back to the future by mistake.

When the ceremony was done, the bishop remained where he was, talking with the villagers, forgiving each of them individually for their sins, as he had done at MacGregor Castle a few days earlier.

Cam looked around him, surprised to see Rachel had slipped away. He followed her outside, finding her standing by a thin stream that ran around the edge of the range.

"This is the kitchen," she said when he caught up with her. "Remember that night we spent together here?"

He nodded. "How could I forget?"

"I knew then," she said quietly. "That I loved you, I mean. I tried to deny it, even to myself but there was no denying the truth."

"What's that?" he asked, looking at her outstretched hand.

"The key to the box," she replied. "Let it go and it becomes the key in the loch. I will never look at the necklace again. It feels like an important moment. Let it go now and I stay here forever, never get the chance to see my mom again."

"Maybe-"

Before he could say another word she'd let go. The key fell into the stream. The current caught it at once. Despite its weight it didn't sink to the bottom, instead floating away out of sight into the darkness. "Maybe what?" she asked, turning to look at him, a single tear running down her cheek.

"Maybe we should join the others."

"In a minute," she replied.

He slipped an arm around her and together they looked out into the darkness.

Somewhere out there the key was slipping and sliding into the loch. It would sink to the bottom of the dark water minutes later, remaining hidden for many years until the currents swirled and it slowly shifted, edging toward the shore.

Centuries would pass before it reached the beach, buried under sand, waiting for a child running along the beach to trip over it.

That child would pick it up and take it home with her. From there it would make its way, slowly, over many years, to an antique shop in New York. There it would remain until a buyer was found. A buyer who knew exactly what she was looking for.

Cam and Rachel didn't know anything about what would happen to the key in the loch. They didn't know what would happen to the other five keys. Five keys that unlocked five doors to the past. Five stories waiting to be told.

The story of Cam and Rachel was almost over. There was just one chapter left to tell and that came two years after their return to MacGregor Castle.

Chapter Twenty

Rachel couldn't believe what she was seeing. "How is this even possible?" she asked, looking from Cam to the alchemist and back again. "I can't believe it."

"Believe it," Cam replied. "Thomas has done it."

She looked down at the table, hardly able to move. "And you're sure it will work."

"Aye," Thomas said, running his hand through his shock of gray hair. "It has taken many a sleepless night but I think I've managed it."

She picked up the cellphone, hardly willing to hope.

A length of oil coated twine ran from it to a glass bottle filled with a dark liquid. From that bottle a mass of metal ran to other tubes and pipes. Liquids swirled and bubbled. Heat rose from the fire in the corner of the room, the flames powering the whole thing. An entire room given over to one task.

"You have made a battery?"

"Of sorts," Thomas said. "It harnesses heat as power but I dinnae ken how long it will give you. Minutes maybe. Perhaps only seconds."

"Any time is long enough," she replied, taking a deep breath. "Are we all ready?"

"Do it," Cam said.

"I pray it works," Thomas added, wincing as she pressed the power button. He let out a gasp as the cellphone beeped in response, powering up at once.

Rachel's hands shook as she tapped on the screen, loading the last number that called her and redialling it.

The line was crackly. Low battery beeps were constant, the screen fading and then returning to life. Each time it died, she held her breath. Thomas pumped the bellows and it came back stronger.

However long she had, hopefully it would be long enough for one final talk with her mother.

There was a series of dial tones and then a click

as the cellphone connected. "Who is this?" Morag asked. "Rachel, is that you?"

"It's me, Mom," Rachel said. "I love you."

"How are you calling me?"

"We got the cellphone to work but I don't know how long it will last. I miss you Mom. I never got to say bye properly. I'm sorry."

"You'll see me again soon."

"I will?"

"I just have to catch a flight. There's an antique shop I need to visit. Then I'll be able to come and see you."

"I'm married, Mom. And I'm pregnant too. We're going to have a baby, me and Cam."

A louder beep from the cellphone, the call almost dying. Morag's voice was faint, fading all the time. "Your father would have been so proud. Make sure you-"

The line went dead. She looked at Thomas but he only shook his head. "It was all I could give you, I'm sorry."

She managed a smile through her tears. "It was enough. I thank you for your hard work."

"It was nothing," he said with a shrug.

"Nothing?" Cam said. "Och, I observed you up night after night. You have done much for both of us, more than you realize. You will be handsomely rewarded."

Thomas excused himself, leaving her alone with Cam. "I miss her," she managed to say between her tears.

"You will see her again," he replied, holding her tight to his chest.

"Will I?"

"She said so herself."

Rachel wanted to believe it but it was hard. For so many years she had wondered who her mother was and now she knew. It seemed too cruel for her to find her only to have her snatched away in the same instant.

She put her hand on her belly, drawing comfort from the thought of the new life growing in there. Cam's hand slid over her own. "Our wee bairn," he said quietly.

"What should we call him?"

"It's a he, is it?" Cam replied. "You're sure of that?"

"I just know it's a he and he needs a name. How about Philip?"

"I like that."

She slid the cellphone into her pocket despite somehow knowing it would never work again. It was her last connection to her own time and she felt that call had been not just saying goodbye to her mother but saying goodbye to the twenty-first century.

From now on she was a medieval Highland lass, and that meant enjoying the celebrations with the rest of them. She would hold onto the slip of paper with the word 'love' written on it. That would be enough.

It was the anniversary of Cam's marriage to Rachel and almost the entire clan was freed from work for the day. Only the guards remained at their post, the rest indulging in a great feast taking place in the courtyard. Tables had been moved outside for the occasion. People were sitting, drinking ale, laughing, talking loudly.

Later, there would be dancing. First, there was much eating to be done. Rachel wiped away her tears as she joined her husband at the top table. Philip stood beside them, pounding the butt of his knife on the tabletop. "Quiet," he shouted. "I have something to say."

"Make it quick," someone shouted back. "It'll be winter soon."

"My speeches aren't usually that long, are they?"

A groan in response.

"Right, well I'll keep this one as short as I can. There is peace in the Highlands like none we have ever known." He paused, looking out at the crowd. "This peace has come at a high price. Castles lay empty. Villages are no more than waste. Food is scarce in many places still.

"But there is hope. Crops grow once more. The land is freed from darkness and there is one reason for that above all others. These two people here saved us all. To them, raise your drinks high. Cam and Rachel." He held up his goblet as the tribute echoed around the courtyard.

"Cam and Rachel."

"Speech!" someone called out, waving at Cam.

He stood up, waiting for silence. "I thank you all for your kindness. This clan only exists because of the people in it, people who are capable of great good and great evil.

"The choices we make have ripples that pass down through the ages. I have chosen a bride and together we shall have a child. Who knows where that child will go in life. Or their children. All I know is that I am glad they will have better chances because the evil that threatened to consume us is gone from our land."

He paused for a moment, waiting for the cheering to die down. "We must continue to be vigilant," he said when he could make himself heard once more.

"Darkness waits always at the edge of our vision. We must watch for it. We must be the light. We must be the beacon the Highlands can see at every hour of night and day. All our children need us to watch out for them until we are old and broken and then they will, in turn, watch out for us. I raise my cup not to me and my wife but to all of you. To the MacGregors. May God watch over us all."

"The MacGregors!" The noise was so loud that the crows on the towers took off in alarm.

Cam sat back down as the conversation resumed around the courtyard. Rachel looked at him, seeing in his eyes a joy that was tempered with concern for his clan. "To think they almost burned us alive," she said, shaking her head slowly. "It's strange to think how easily they were swayed."

"It wasn't easy to turn this lot," Cam replied. "Tor had his work cut out dripping his poison, telling them lies. Even with the barefoot man's help, he didn't succeed."

"Came close though."

"Aye but what matters is we're alive and all is well once more."

The meal went on long after dark. Rachel was glad when it was over, much as she enjoyed it. The longer her pregnancy progressed, the more tired she felt. She would be glad when her son was finally born and she could sleep on her front again.

She couldn't say how she knew he was going to be a boy. Heir to the MacGregor clan. That was a strange thought.

She yawned when Cam finally led her into his bed chamber. The Laird was supposed to sleep alone but Cam had no time for such arcane rules. He slept every night beside Rachel and she was glad.

She felt at her safest with him wrapped around her, knowing he would protect her from any danger that might arise in the night. It was a good feeling.

She lay in bed after the feast. Smoke still drifted from the recently snuffed candles as she thought about the phone call she'd made.

She had spoken to her mother. It was all too brief but she knew she should not be bitter about that. She had a chance to speak to her across a great distance and across the centuries. How her cellphone connected, she had no idea.

What she didn't know was that centuries before Morag's birth, her ancestors had inherited a tiny amount of magic without even realizing it was happening. That magic passed down the family for generations until Rachel was born. It was that magic that allowed the call to connect her to Morag,

The cellphone would never work again. It would eventually be buried deep under the castle for some future archeologist to scratch their head over.

Rachel no longer needed it. She had all she needed in the room with her. "Your grandmother is going to come and visit you," she said quietly while stroking her bump.

Behind her Cam stirred and then woke. "What's wrong?" he asked, alert at once.

"Nothing," she replied, closing her eyes and yawning again as she drifted off to sleep. "Nothing at all."

Outside, snow began to fall, blanketing the castle courtyard in white. The guards shivered at their posts, stamping their feet to keep warm.

It would be a long, hard winter.

Epilogue

Three years later...

The children were asleep. Morag in the cot, Philip across in his wee bed. Cam was in bed asleep. Rachel would soon join him but she couldn't resist looking at her children for a little while first.

Rachel looked down at the cot, unable to stop smiling. Morag was so bonny she thought she might burst.

Two children. Morag and Philip. Named for her mother and Cam's mentor. The births had been nothing compared to what she was expecting. She looked down at her scrunched up face as she shifted in her sleep.

She remembered her fear concerning the first delivery, how a lack of modern medicine meant any birth was a risk. There was no ambulance to race her off to a hospital. The nearest they had was the clan midwife, Old Sue.

Old Sue had listened when Rachel talked about cleanliness. She might not understand why but when she insisted the towels were boil washed, the servants did it. No one disobeyed Old Sue.

It had been three years since Rachel had slipped back in time to medieval Scotland. In that time she'd learned to love the place so much, her memories of the twenty-first century were fading. Having children meant her whole focus was on being a wife and mother, not on regretting life without hairdryers or Kindles.

Many things made her happy in the Highlands. Looking in at her sleeping baby was one. Turning to see little Philip asleep in his bed was another. Then there was Cam. Waking every morning next to her husband was a pleasure that would never fade.

There was only one thing that gnawed at her. She had hoped to see her mother again but it hadn't happened.

She had so much to tell her. She wanted to show her the grandchildren she'd never had the chance to meet. She yearned for the chance to introduce the two of them to their grandmother but, as each day ticked by, it seemed less and less likely.

Once she was certain her family were all asleep, she left the bed chamber, descending the stairs to the courtyard with a lantern in her hand.

She crossed the open space quickly, a chill wind blowing straight through her cloak. Winter was on the way. It would be her third one in the Middle Ages. She had gotten used to the snow and the ice, but the wind still chilled her to the bone when it struck, no matter how many layers of clothing she wore.

She was glad to get inside the chapel. Though not warm, it was infinitely preferable to the icy blast outside. She would not stay long. Soon she would be back in her warm bedchamber. It was time to give thanks once again. Give thanks and ask once again for the one thing that would make her family feel complete.

Morag might wake and need feeding at any moment and Cam had not slept much the night before, needed to deal with a border dispute over by MacKenzie territory. Grumblings were once again building between the two clans.

It seemed that peace could only last so long before darkness began to swirl once more. How long until the Highlands could relax? They had the Jacobite Rebellion to come, the Highland Clearances, and losing at one World Cup after another. Maybe she should introduce soccer to them? Get them practising early. The thought made her smile.

She knelt by the altar, closing her eyes to mutter the same silent prayer she said every night. "Please keep my family safe, Lord. Please look after the clan. Please let me speak to my mother one more time."

Her family was safe. The clan was safe. The final wish was yet to be granted. Would it ever come true?

Behind her the door to the chapel creaked open. She stood up, wondering if Cam had come looking for her. Did he wonder where she went each night before bed?

It wasn't Cam who stood there.

It was Morag.

"Mom!" Rachel ran to her, throwing her arms around her.

Morag held her close, not saying anything for a very long time. They wept together, Rachel not sure if she was dreaming. Was it really her? It was. It truly was.

Later, they sat together by the altar, talking quietly.

"How did you get here?" Rachel asked. "I never thought I'd see you again."

"I've been doing some research," Morag replied. "For years none of it made sense but now it's starting to. I had one chance to save you and it worked."

"What worked?"

"There are six keys in total, six keys to the past. We've been using the same one, you and me. It took you into the future and saved you from the fire. It was the same one that brought me back. The necklace doesn't matter. It's the key that matters, the key that was in the loch, the key that must go back into the loch no matter what the future holds. The key decides when to be found. That's what matters, not the necklace."

"I don't understand," Rachel said. "The necklace sent you forward in time, surely? Without it that wound would have killed you."

"It was the key, reaching out through the necklace, like some kind of echo chamber. Know what else I found? There are five more keys out there somewhere."

"How do you know? Where did they come from, the keys, I mean? Who made them?"

"I don't know. I couldn't find out. There are pictures of them in all kinds of books, collectors offering insane amounts of money for them. I think some people know what they do. I think some people would kill to get their hands on them."

"Are you in danger? Are we?" She thought about someone attacking her family over the key. The idea made her shudder.

Morag smiled. "No, nothing like that. I think the keys can look after themselves. I lost our one coming back and that's okay. It slipped out of my hand and into the loch. It's done its job and I thank it and its creator. We can be together."

"Aye. So we can."

"How are you finding the Middle Ages? You're starting to sound pretty Scottish."

"Am I? Well, I do feel like I belong here."

"You do belong here. You were born here."

"In Scotland?"

"In the Middle Ages as you call it. Only for me and the rest of the clan, this is the present day."

Rachel frowned. "I'm not sure I understand."

"You went into the past. I went into the future. I was given a key as a keepsake by my parents when I was little. They never told me what it could do. When you were very young our village was attacked and burned. The key was ready. I got one of the villagers to use it. All of a sudden I knew what it would do. It just came to me in a flash. He pushed you through the door and into the future because the key let him. That way you and your brother would be safe."

"Have you seen him? Alan I mean?"

Morag looked sad. "I tried. He wouldn't believe I was his mother. Kept telling me I was a liar out to steal his inheritance from him. I gave up in the end. He will realize eventually and then, if he's meant to join us, he will."

Rachel could tell she was leaving a lot unsaid but she didn't press the matter. There would be time enough to talk more in the future.

"Your father died in that fire," Morag continued. "He was a good man and I know he'd be so proud of all that you've done."

"What was he like?"

"Tall, so strong, he had a laugh that could make the whole house shake and he laughed a lot. He could use his sword like no one else but his wit was faster."

They talked further, the night passing by until Rachel suddenly realized how long she'd been away from her children. "I better head back," she said. "But I've got so much more to ask you. How did you end up trapped on the island? How did you learn magic? What did you think of the future?"

"Time to talk about all those things in the morning. For now, I want to see my grandchild."

"Grandchildren."

"You mean you had twins?"

"No but I've had a second child."

"You have? Boy or girl?"

"Come and see for yourself."

"You can't do that. Tell me!"

"I've waited thirty years for this and you can't wait three minutes?"

"Hmm. We better be quick."

When they got to the keep Rachel was surprised to hear Cam's voice coming from the great hall. She stuck her head in from the corridor. "All okay?" she asked.

Cam was deep in conversation with a man in the MacKenzie tartan. "All is well," he replied before waving the man away, "We will talk more in a moment."

The man bowed and retreated, leaving Cam with his family. "The maid watches the children," he said as they joined him. "The border dispute grows fiercer."

"A Laird's work is never done," Morag said.

Cam looked at her with fresh eyes, realizing who it was. "I thought I recognized you. Morag! You survived then? What are you doing here?"

"I've come back to join my family. If you'll have me, of course."

"Of course." He got to his feet, leading the way out into the corridor. He paused to talk to the MacKenzie man on the way. "I will be back shortly."

The man bowed once again. Cam then walked up the stairs to the bedchamber. Morag followed and Rachel brought up the rear, not sure if she was dreaming. She hoped not. It would be too cruel to be given this moment only for it to be taken away once more.

At the doorway to the bedchamber, they all stopped. Morag took a quiet step in first, nodding a greeting to the maid who smiled back.

Rachel smiled as her mother leaned over the

bed, looking down at little Morag. "She's so beauti-ful," she whispered, turning to look at Cam and Rachel. "She looks too precious for words." She looked across at Philip who was laid on his side, breathing steadily, unaware of all the attention.

After a moment longer, Morag returned to the doorway, tears rolling down her cheeks. "I'm so glad I got to see them both," she said. "You have made an old woman very happy indeed."

"Come," Cam said. "You will sleep in the garret beside us."

He had the maid prepare the bed while he finished with the emissary from the MacKenzies. While he was gone, Rachel fed little Morag who had woken grumbling for food. By the time she was done, Cam was done and her mother was settled in her room. Rachel bid her goodnight before joining Cam in bed.

She settled down to sleep, so happy she felt she might cry again. Her joy only faded when she fell asleep. She dreamed of the future.

Her children were grown up. Philip was a man and something bad was coming for him, something she couldn't see but she knew it was there even though he didn't.

She tried to warn him but he couldn't hear her

shouts. He stood looking every inch the Highland warrior as she yelled a warning at the top of her voice. No sound came out. He heard nothing.

She awoke with a start, sitting up in bed. "Just a dream," she said out loud, climbing out of bed and looking down at her son who slept on oblivious to her concerns. "Just a dream."

What would life be like for him when he grew up? Was the dream an omen of things to come?

She returned to bed, settling once more with Cam instinctively draping his arm over her. Her family was together. That was what mattered. The future wasn't written yet.

It was just a dream. Nothing bad was going to happen.

She slept once again and this time she didn't dream.

The next day she woke up with her family near her. The man she loved was by her side. He would remain by her side and in her heart for the rest of their lives.

The End

Want to know if Tor is brought to justice?

Want to find out if the barefoot man really is gone forever?

Sign up for my mailing list and get all the answers in an exclusive bonus epilogue.

Sign up here.

Author's Note

This is the first story in the MacGregor Clan series.

The second book, The Key in the Door, stars their son, Eddard, and Morag and is set around the start of the thirteenth century.

The Key to Her Heart features the son of Eddard and Morag, and is mostly set in and around 1240.

The Key to Her Past stars Wallace and Natalie and is set in and around 1270.

MacGregor Castle is fictional but I have tried to make it as realistic as possible regarding the time period.

The fifth book in the series is due out around October 2019. Sign up to my newsletter here to be the first to find out more.

Made in the USA
Monee, IL
17 September 2019